The Man From Düsseldorf

A Tribute to Claus Laufenburg

Edited by
Brendan Connell

SNUGGLY BOOKS

Contents

The Man From Düsseldorf

Quentin S. Crisp

Who Is Claus Laufenburg?

GOD alone knows what year it was—the years go by so quickly now. It might as well have been the Middle Ages, although the wretch is not yet dead. I speak of Crispin L. Quaint, christened into obscurity; given a name already taken; a name already taken by a gay raconteur whose gospel was: to be your one and only self.

It was a Monday afternoon—the rest we must pick up as we go along. Crispin, at his desk, was dallying somewhere between duties and desires, when he received an e-mail from Claus Laufenburg. His indecision was resolved—to read an e-mail from Claus Laufenburg was both duty and desire. He clicked on it.

Dear Crispin,

Your signed collection, *The Ritual Disembowelment of My Sick Mind*, lies mere inches from my left hand. Soon that same left hand will join the right in parting those pages and disclosing the delightful words they enfold to my waiting eyes, which will in turn relay those words to my brain, which will translate them—I fully expect and have no significant doubts on this matter—into an incomparable literary experience.

But more on that later. I am writing today with a humble offer that I hope might be of interest to you. Just let me know. It is in my power to secure you a place (+1) on the guest list at tonight's performance by Momus. If you are free and of a mind to attend, by all means simply reply to this e-mail in the affirmative. There is an ear—I will not say to whom it is attached—into which I will speak the necessary word, and all will be arranged without the least shadow of trouble.

I look forward to your reply,

Yours,

Claus

Crispin wrote an immediate reply.

Dear Claus,

Many thanks for your missive.

Once more April is upon us, and spring would not be spring without my attendance at the annual Momus UK performance. It is, for me, as cherry blossom.

Your e-mail, then, is indescribably timely. You see, various misfortunes had kept me from noticing the date of the show this year until all tickets were gone. You can imagine my dismay when I discovered this—I have no time to describe it accurately, I'm afraid—and my gladness now on opening your e-mail and finding the situation repaired.

I must therefore most gratefully accept your kind offer in the hope that I might someday—retroactively—deserve it. For now, I must bow to fate and say yes.
Yours unworthily, etc.,
Crispin

Crispin clicked send. In suspense, he was unable to focus his mind on anything else until the confirmation came from Claus, seven minutes later, that his name (+1) was now on the list. The relief occasioned at this was in itself so overwhelming that Crispin decided it was necessary to finish work for the day in order to recuperate.

Crispin's mood was spoilt somewhat by the fact that he was unable to find a +1 to accompany him. Still, he mused, as he ascended towards the familiar exit from Dalston Junction Station, for a writer solitary thought, observation, sensation, must take the place of company for the greater part of life.

He crossed to the other side of the street and slipped down Ashwin Road. Soon the glass frontage of Café OTO, next to the Arcola Theatre, was before him, like a transparent page waiting to be written on with the experiences of the evening. It was, for Crispin, at this stage of his life, a palimpsest page, on which the ghosts of older, half-effaced writings were visible beneath the supposed blank of the present.

With appropriate solemnity, he approached and crossed the threshold.

"Quaint. Crispin Quaint." He announced himself to someone sitting at a desk just inside the entrance. She searched a list on the crumpled printout and, taking a blue biro, drew a line through his name when she found it.

"What about your plus-one?" she asked.

"Oh, she's running late. Is it okay if she just gives my name when she arrives?"

"Sure thing," said the doorperson, and made a note on the printout.

"Thank you. That's most kind."

Quaint now turned dutifully to the bar. Strong Pavlovian imprinting reminded him that the prices of the drinks here were painful, but since admission had been free he could pretend he was buying himself the ticket with the first couple of drinks, and still tell himself he had obtained entry cheaply. His third drink he could imagine, financially speaking, to be his first, by which time the first two actual drinks should have softened the blow a little. He exhaled, nodded, and proceeded with this plan.

With the hit to his debit card duly taken, and with gaseous lager in hand, Crispin wandered away to find a vantage point from which to view the stage—the stage being simply an area of the floor of Café OTO surrounded by folding chairs. Most of the chairs were taken by now, so he stationed himself with his back to the wall, sipped at the insipid beverage, and waited.

The performance had not started, and Crispin had got close to the bottom of his glass in sips and gulps, when, a little to his surprise, he was hailed by a figure approaching from his left. In a moment, however, his surprise vanished. He recognized the newcomer as John Worley, also a regular at these annual performances, and someone who Crispin knew by chance from an entirely different milieu—the milieu of the genre fiction on which Crispin had managed to piggyback for his first few publications. John had spoken to Crispin many years ago at a more or less literary event and, confessing to having read some of Crispin's work, had made some guardedly appreciative comments in whose midst he had unfortunately, at some point, inserted the word "old-fashioned." The next day, Crispin had written a two-thousand-word blog entry describing the incident and defending himself from the imputation. They had subsequently met at another more or less literary event where much awkwardness had ensued until all the awkwardness—or the most prominent portion of it—had been painstakingly interrogated into some manageable new equilibrium.

The two now began pre-gig small talk, which was not easy, since Crispin sensed that John was an intensely private, almost secretive person—probably the kind of person, thought Crispin, who would be good at espionage. Then, out of nowhere, as it seemed, something occurred to him that he thought might open up the conversation a little.

"Do you know Claus?"

"Claus?"

"Claus Laufenburg?"

"No. Who's that?"

For some reason, Crispin found himself utterly bewildered by this response.

"Claus. Claus Laufenburg. You know."

"I don't know anyone. And no one knows me."

"Ah . . . for some reason . . . I thought . . ."

But Crispin was unable to complete the sentence, so decided to change direction:

"So, how up to date are you with the Momus catalogue?"

Neither of them, it seemed, had the last three albums, and it was agreed that assimilating all of the copious Momus output was no easy task. The conversation ended when Crispin went to the bar for his second pint. It was not resumed on his return, and before long the ectomorphic Momus, with eyepatch in place and, as it seemed, permanently arched eyebrow, took the stage, as long-shanked a figure as the stretching shadow of a pantomime of the phrase "on the trail of," and the time for conversation was past. In keeping with past occasions, Momus was as waspish, playful and paper-delicate in his performance as an origami wasps' nest. Crispin was aware of cerebral, sensory and even a degree of emotional intoxication. Momus's one-man am-dram vaudeville presentation was tempered by an otherworldly wistfulness that sometimes was capable of leading the listener beneath the stalactites of *sehnsucht* deep into the dripping, shadowy cave of the soul's forgotten delights. Crispin made sure to store the best of these moments in his own personal noösphere, to be drawn upon later, as needed, for his writing.

When Momus got to what had become almost his signature tune, "Beowulf (I Am Deformed)," Crispin knew that the performance was reaching its climax. Soon it would be time for the encore. Crispin decided to lubricate the sliding slope to the end of the night with another drink.

On some previous occasions, he had been able to talk to Momus a little after the show, but a kind of melancholy satisfaction with tonight's performance made him decide that he would not crowd and compete this time with the other fans, diffident and eager, with whom Momus would make conversation like a cornered swashbuckler.

However, not long after Crispin had made this fortifying resolution and applauded the last song of the encore, he went outside to finish his fourth pint in the air of the spring evening and found himself unexpectedly drawn into conversation with a number of others who had also been in the audience. There was a tall young fellow with a mop of curly hair on top, and a slightly shorter young fellow with straight, silky hair, and a young lady with a kind of unguarded immediacy to her manner who looked younger than both of them.

"Do you know Momus, too?" asked the shorter of the young men.

By this time Crispin was feeling a little hazy and he was not sure what had given this impression. Perhaps it had simply come to the attention of the three young people that many of the audience might "know Momus," and this question might therefore be their testing of a hypothesis, or a subtle means of networking, giving him a pretext to make known his own position in the constellation of which Momus was one of the brighter stars. Crispin allowed himself, therefore, with a little too much of gladness, to succumb to gravity and slip into their orbit.

"Oh, not really. I mean, I interviewed him some time back, which I imagine he might recall if you asked, but I'm not one of the people he wrote songs for on *Stars Forever*. I wish I had been, but I simply couldn't scrape the money together in time. When I'd come out of the medical trials I'd gone through to stump up the cash, I looked at the website again, but by then all the places had gone to others."

"Oh, I love that album!" exclaimed the young lady.

Crispin would have liked the opportunity to scrutinize her more closely. For some reason he found her enthusiasm incongruous when its object was the music of the, as it were, irony-embalmed, cult-status elder statesman of pop-lyric debauchery.

More drinks were bought and conversation continued. It soon transpired that the young lady—Isabella by name—was Momus's assistant, whatever that entailed. In any case, she was clearly a fan, and her readiness to express her admiration without restraint or affectation was genuinely charming and unusual. Such young blood was keeping the music of Momus alive, no doubt. Crispin could not help reflecting on his own position as—what? An artist? A creative? Had he even managed to break through the wall of embarrassment that anyone attempting to go the distance must encounter? It seemed to him, rather, that he had hit the wall, and that it stretched car-toonishly around him, and he was stuck in it, writhing and wriggling, like a fly in a web.

He found himself questioning Isabella with deep interest regarding her opinion on "Bishonen" and one or two other songs from the same album. When she questioned him, in turn, on his favorite songs, unable to think of anything safe in time, he haplessly divulged, "Ventriloquists and Dolls."

More drinks were bought.

The conversation between the four of them took on a hectic tone. Everything appeared to Crispin to be going unusually well. He had a sense of real camaraderie with these strangers. They seemed to find his wit piquant, his observations novel and penetrating.

"Crispin *L.* Quaint," he heard himself saying at one point. "Look, my passport, see?" He fished it from his inside pocket and showed the assembled.

"Did you change your name?" asked the tall young man, Michael.

"No. I am the real Quaint. The other one was just born first. This is important. If you look me up on the internet later, you'll know who I am, and someday you'll remember this conversation."

"Why?" asked Michael. "Are you planning some kind of spectacular mass-murder?"

"H a h a h a h a h a h a h a h a h a h a h a h a h a h a . H a h a h a h a h a h a h a h a h a h a h a h a h a h a . Hahahahahaha."

Crispin was aware he was laughing a little too much.

"No, I won't be doing murders or any criminal activity of that sort. Hahahahahaha. I'm thinking of something quite different."

Crispin remembered little after this except that the four temporary friends soon dispersed. Was there a hint of shame in this swift diaspora? He only recalled shouting sorrowfully as he approached the station alone: "You don't understand art! I'm an honorary gay! I'm here to embarrass the wooooorrrlldd!"

The next morning, memories of the preceding night trailed patterns of unease through his general wooziness. He ate a Danish pastry, crammed some Ibuprofen into his mouth, and washed it down with Earl Grey, the bergamot almost making him vomit. Crawling once more beneath the duvet, he lay abed some time in agony. At about three o'clock, hunger began to get the better of him; he decided there was no avoiding the day, after all. He struggled through a bowl of leek soup from a tin, logged on to the internet and, finding no messages for him, Googled his name. To his considerable surprise, there was an item in the search results that he had not seen before—what's more, it was a review. Of *The Ritual Disembowelment of My Sick Mind*. By Spencer Gladyawn. At the *Gatekeeper* website. However, the headline was not very auspicious, he thought: "A Curious Cure for Cerebral Constipation." Taking a breath he clicked . . . and read.

This new collection of semi-autobiographical fiction and autobiographical essays from Crispin L. Quaint—who has apparently largely given up on the attempt to be creative—sadly gives the lie to the old saying that truth is stranger than fiction. Quaint's fiction is stranger than his self-confessed life, but predictably so, and reading of his life makes it all too clear why he would strain to invent such transparent fictions in the first place.

As the above suggests, I am of that breed of *rara avis* who has already some acquaintance with Quaint—sadly not the kind of *rara avis* to excite any well adjusted ornithologist. Perhaps a decade back, there were enough people on the fringes of the fringes of the shadowy world of contemporary fiction who scented some exciting aroma of *sui generis* in Quaint's prose to awaken an interest in others outside the coterie. But though the name Quaint still lingers in corners like stale smoke, the flame has gone out.

It was worse than he had anticipated. He could not read on. One might wait half a lifetime or more for a review in the *Gatekeeper*, and then . . . Well, for Quaint that "and then" had come. What could he hope for now? This was one of those occasional bone-shaking blows that jolts a writer out of his own identity into the nausea of being nobody, from which he might never recover. His instinct to avoid this day had been well founded. Feeling sicker than ever, he went back to bed.

Just after nightfall, having gained some degree of equilibrium through deep and solitary communion with self-pity, he re-emerged from beneath the bed covers and sent off a wounded but artful e-mail to the poet Rupert Asher. He apologized for his recent silence, suggested they meet soon in the usual branch of Starbucks for a catch-up over beverages, enquired after Rupert's writing life and, as if it were an afterthought, near the very end of the e-mail, inserted a link to Spencer Gladyawn's review and made a remark that perhaps, after all, Gladyawn was right, and Crispin should consider some other avenue to walk in life than that of author.

Two bleak hours and thirty-seven arduous minutes passed before he received a reply. Rupert was free this Thursday afternoon and would be delighted to meet up. As for Spencer Gladyawn: "There are few people alive today," Asher proclaimed, "who have done as much as he has to ensure that the literary life of this country is a non-event. You should consider his scorn a badge of honor. You're a writer—there's no escaping it. We can't look back. We just have to keep on writing and putting it out there. Don't worry about good or bad. Just follow your destiny."

When Crispin arrived at the branch of Starbucks on St. Martin's Lane, he first looked for Rupert's beret, and having spotted it—Rupert was always there first, as if he was a man not of arrivals or departures, but of pre-existent presence—went to the counter to order a cappuccino and examine the confectionaries. He took his drink and the chocolate brownie he had settled on to the table at which Rupert was ensconced. The latter looked up at his approach, having been apparently absorbed in writing. A pad lay open on the table, the lines of half a page filled with a handwritten brew of sensibility and vocabulary in purple ink, like the unfolding leaves of some unheard-of tea.

"Ah, hello Crispin," came a voice as hooked and soothing as the tongue of a cat. "How have you been? Time speeds by. I hope you're still being creative as usual."

Crispin took the chair opposite Rupert at the little table and soon they settled into another installment of their digressive and unconcluding conversation, making sallies into recent reading, sifting through reflections on and recommendations of obscure authors, perching for a moment or two on shop talk, swooping into gossip pertaining to certain names in the worlds of music and of letters, reminiscing wistfully on the pop culture of past decades, comparing inspirations and fascinations.

"I had a book back from the Romanian publisher you told me about," Rupert was saying. "Beautifully done. I can see he has marvelous taste. As for the rest, it's best not to ask questions. Send in your writing, take the money—it's not as if we ever get much of that, anyway—and let posterity do the rest. In fifty years or so no one will care about the controversies. If anything, they'll add a little color to the literary histories, to remind academics who have never done anything creative in their lives that they don't move in the same world as the people they write about."

"Yes . . . yes . . ." said Crispin doubtfully. He was still smarting from the Gladyawn review and far from confident that posterity—assuming there would be such a thing for anyone fifty years hence—would show him any kindness at all.

"As writers we have to live a pirate lifestyle," Rupert continued. "We've no choice, really, and it's probably for the best, anyway. Raise the flag. Bring a little excitement. None of that boring PC rubbish."

Pirates? What did that remind him of? *Feel like slitting my wrist when I Google myself these days—most of the results are just pirate copies of my books. Copyright. Sampling. Eyepatch. Momus. Oh yes, but it's different for musicians—at least they can get paid for live performance. Momus. Live.*

Memories of the preceding Monday night began to resurface, which had been temporarily eclipsed by the Gladyawn agony. Among the memories, mixed in with the swirling spirals of shame, of aesthetic satisfaction and of quotidian wretchedness, was a warm and fragrant trail of unusual intrigue. He remembered speaking to John Worley and the strangeness around the name of Claus Laufenburg.

"By the way," he blurted, impelled into speech, "you know Claus, don't you? Claus Laufenburg."

"Claus, oh yes. We go back a long way. There really wouldn't be a scene today without Claus."

"Who is he?"

Rupert stared at him for a while. Crispin thought perhaps he should rephrase the question but suddenly felt entirely incapable of doing so.

"I don't know," said Rupert at last, in a faint, faraway voice.

After a silence he resumed his previous theme, developing it, eventually, into a panegyric on the life and work of Joe Meek.

As if the pursuit of intrigue might in some way act as a balm for the injury done to his sense of personhood, Crispin applied himself with unhabitual energy to a series of separate e-mails addressed to friends and acquaintances either known for some kind of artistic talent or who were shameless facilitators of such. He concocted a boilerplate e-mail which made, as if incidentally, towards the end, an enquiry regarding the addressee's knowledge of Claus Laufenburg, and he adjusted the e-mail's details for each person he sent it to. As the replies came back to him over the following days and weeks, what he had suspected nonetheless became an increasing—not diminishing—surprise: every single one of them knew of Claus Laufenburg.

"And yet John Worley . . ." Crispin pondered to himself.

But with expected surprise came an unexpected surprise. Crispin's gambit had been this: He wanted, he wrote, to send Claus a gift, but did not want to alert him to this intention by asking him for his current address. "You wouldn't happen to have it by any chance?"

Each correspondent wrote back obligingly with an address; each address was different.

✭

Crispin found it hard to think only in his head and since he feared to think out loud, anticipating this would be as welcome to others as halitosis, he did most of his thinking with pen on paper, thereby committing a great many indiscretions to the page. What a strange world it was—he reflected—that this blundering, shrinking spirit of his, which necessitated such a course of action, had occasionally even been called brave. There were in the world, then, people even more confused than he.

Since deep thought was now required, he bought a new notepad. Across its cover he scrawled the title he had given it, indicating its function: *Book of Mysteries*. Sitting at his desk, he turned to the first page of the notepad and wrote the day's date. Beneath this he wrote the following question:

Who is Claus Laufenburg?

He sat. With his hand to his mouth he continued to scrutinize the question he had just written and, indeed, this went on for a considerable length of time. Then, apparently enlivened by the advent of an idea, he put pen to paper again and wrote, three lines below his first question:

Who is John Worley?

He nodded and seemed to chew his own mouth in thought. Then he laid down his pen.

It was important to be patient in such matters, he decided. As someone had once said, the art of writing—and therefore of thinking—was the art of applying bum to seat. He looked at the time and set an alarm on his phone to go off in another hour. Then he sat and stared at the page, and waited.

After some nights of this, he decided it might be just as well to outsource the problem. Searching through his virtual address book, he settled on the name he thought most appropriate—someone who knew everyone, someone whose influence spanned continents, someone who reverence had prevented him from writing to the first time: Kim Newman.

He composed an e-mail. It was risky, of course, as he didn't know Newman that well, but since he stated near the beginning that he understood his correspondent to be near omniscient in such matters, he hoped the latter would be somewhat disarmed and put his knowledge at Crispin's disposal.

After this opening gambit, he laid out the information he had gathered and tried to give some idea of the weird shadows cast by these fragments of mystery on the walls of his mind without sounding too much like a goat-eyed crackpot.

"I would be immensely grateful, then," he concluded, "for any information you might have relating to these odd circumstances that might help to ease my perplexity. In full appreciation of your worldly discretion and sensitivity to the subtleties of this, our realm of phantoms, rumors, glamors and bewilderments, I am most unguardedly yours . . ." etc.

He wondered if the ending was a little too much, but could not bring himself to tone it down. Taking a fatalistic breath, he clicked send.

How long would it take someone like Kim Newman to reply? Since there was no one like Kim Newman it was impossible to say.

Crispin felt that, in sending the e-mail, he had done something irrecoverable, and he did not even know what. If and when his unearthly suspense would end was also a matter hidden beyond clouds of obscurity.

He had been toying, recently, with a bildungsroman under the title of *No one Asked the Gibbous Boy*. But 'toying' was not the right word. He had been drawn to those feelings, those events, those dizzy aspirations that had formed his first impulses to write, from which he felt he had long strayed, this way and that, but he was apprehensive that he had left the task too late, that now it required a reconstruction of wounds and wonders that had once been fresh, and so he had dallied, tinkering on the edges of something that daunted him. It was, he feared, a mountain the clambering up of which would be the measure of his whole life; he would discover in the attempt who he truly and finally *was*, whether by failure or success. After sending the e-mail to Newman, he put this novel aside completely.

Maybe he had already failed. His preoccupation with the Gladyawn review suggested this. It was only so fatal to his hopes because he had already come to believe that his hollowed-out heart was hopeless and that it pumped only emptiness and futility to the tips of his talentless fingers.

Rather than write, he began to walk more, and particularly at night when before he had feared ruffians—that they might accost him, skewer his eyeballs, kick him in the kidneys. He still feared them, but walked anyway. He looked for the moon, between the clouds, above the sad rooftops that held in bitter, ignorant lives whose secrets muttered down drainpipes. The moon, that silver soul-mirror so untouched by the griefs and bigotries of this world, perhaps might tell him who he was. A writer he had been, but only by the effort of writing, and since the judgment of history was yet to come and would not come while he lived, he might just as well have been a clown. After all, he was once again only a person, having failed to take wing on his dreams and reach the moon that had set him to dreaming. His worn-out shoes trod the same ground they always had, but his feet were tireder and his heart, like an hourglass whose top half was hope and whose bottom half was disappointment, was now well past the half hour.

Why not, then, simply let it all run away down the gutter? What could he do about it? Let the moon look on, mysterious, aloof, as it had done since before his coming to this world, and let it witness his passing into nothing and make of it what it would. He, Crispin, might be no-body, but if he ceased trying to be for others a somebody, at least he would be his own nobody. Which was to say, logically, nobody's nobody. Well, let it be, then—there was some purity in that to match the moonlight.

But when his spirits had thus ebbed, strange gleams began to flicker in the tide that had near dwindled to its source. After all, these days, even a seemingly hopeless old child such as himself could become puffed up like some fairground-colored balloon with hot air or helium and float up and up above the atmosphere towards its world-orbiting twin. There was still time, and the very point of creativity was to advance the frontier of possibil-ity, was it not?

And sometimes, as his spirit began to turn like this, a smile grew on his face and he became convinced that there had been something providential in the sending of that e-mail to Newman. Its boldness, its strangeness, its tenderness, would be prolific in the alien matrix of Newman's imagination, and there the cells would begin to knit together of a prodigious brainchild. Very probably Newman would have connections in the secret service or some kind of intelligence agency. The two of them would work together to penetrate the heart of the Laufenburg mystery, the tentacles of which, no doubt, reached into many incredible chambers of the unexpected. Of this in-vestigation, much would be born: it would be the belated making of Crispin's character; it would be the crucible of a friendship tinged with cosmic adventure; it would be the source of literary, musical and cinematic spin-offs. The world would open up, at last.

He could picture himself, there in a ski-lodge, high in the Alps, drinking Bénédictine with Newman late in the evening while stars twinkled in an unpolluted sky outside. They would savor in conversational recollection a joint escapade recently completed, and plans for their next would be already afoot. Art thieves in Iran had sold off an ancient fetish into the wrong hands. It needed to be recovered. The rumors surrounding the artifact suggested that, if examined by the right scholars, in correlation with certain other ancient relics, it might change the history books. And he and Newman would be there to see the secrets of antiquity uncovered, and the first two to translate those secrets into a literature that would intoxicate the world.

Sometimes the glow from such thoughts would last until Crispin had returned home, but soon thereafter, doubts would begin to creep in, he would remember what world it was he inhabited, and he would groan in shame and despair.

This period of suspense, self-doubt and solitude was abruptly brought to an end by an e-mail from Kim Newman with the subject heading, "The curious case of Claus Laufenburg." It read as follows:

> Greetings, Mister Quaint,
>   Since the arrival of your recent communication, the contents of which were most interesting, I have been making enquiries

among trusted contacts with the purpose of shedding some light on the mystery you showed such initiative and perspicacity in identifying.

Indeed, I was just last night in close consultation with Marc Almond, David Tibet and Lene Lovich and, piecing together all that we know, we came to the definite conclusion that something is not quite right. In fact, the scale of the not-quite-rightness could be immense, at least, relatively speaking.

Excuse my vagueness—I am writing this in a hurry. We have a plan of action.

Could you send me the e-mail addresses or other contact information of all the people you listed when you last wrote? If there are others you know of who also have any kind of Laufenburg connection, please forward me their details, too. If you can, rank them by trustworthiness, and make sure that none of this comes to the attention of Laufenburg himself.

And Newman proceeded to outline the plan.

The gathering was to be held at the Horse Hospital. It was invitation only, but was disguised as an event in celebration of Count Stenbock. A series of personal calamities had delayed one publisher's release of a deluxe edition of the works of Stenbock and it was thought that a night of arcane ritual and twenty-first century bacchanalia to appease whatever spirits had cursed the project might form a plausible cover story concealing the event's true purpose. Some—including Crispin—feared it would be considered suspicious that Laufenburg had not been invited, but this had been a necessary risk.

The inside of the venue had a peculiar appearance this evening. Its scratchy, post-punk décor, graffitied walls made palimpsest with torn vintage flyers, was designed to be seen in a dim or garish light. Now the lights were up and dustballs were visible and the place had that air of deflation belonging to the aftermath of a party. Moreover, it was full of a curious mix of people who nonetheless seemed to have in common that this kind of dusty aftermath was something like a natural habitat to them.

Kim Newman had taken his place on what passed for a podium, but was conferring in an undertone with Marc Almond away from the microphone. Crispin looked about himself. The crowd was not quite audience-like, as if there were some endless ambiguity to be negotiated between each and all as to who must be a member of the public and who must be a name, who spectator and who spectacle. Crispin recognized, as he knew he would, a large number of personal acquaintances. There were also those he knew of but with whom he had nothing to do. Those entirely unknown to him were probably a minority. There were surprises, too, among the attendees, and one or two of them even pleasant. Upon spying Tommy february6, he took some moments first to believe it and quite a few more to gather courage to approach her and ask for an autograph (perhaps a *faux pas*, he feared, in this crowd).

The murmur grew into a buzz and almost a din as it does on occasions when many are gathered and the starting time and itinerary are uncertain, but eventually, Newman turned to the microphone, tapped it, blew into it, and asked for everybody's attention. When he was satisfied he had it, he began:

"People, unpeople, beautiful ones, others, we who are gathered here, despite our seeming multiplicity, share a single secret, and that secret is the key to a known unknown that joins us. Each of us here is only one degree of separation from each of the others. That degree of separation has a name: Claus Laufenburg. We have come here, then, to ask a single question. And to ask that question, I would like to invite onto the stage the first person to make me see the significance of that question, Mr. Crispin L. Quaint."

Crispin had been told that he would be called up at some point, but he had not realized it would be at the beginning, that his testimony might be a kind of keynote. He made his way with some satisfaction through the crowd, noticing the "who's this fellow then?" looks he was drawing from left and right. After a stumble at the edge of the stage he found his balance and soon stood, rather giddily, in front of the microphone. He hardly dared move his head from side to side to take in these faces from this elevated position.

"Please," prompted Newman, "just read from the *Book of Mysteries* which you mentioned."

"Oh yes," said Crispin, as if coming to himself. From a polythene bag he produced the book he had been asked to bring. He opened it and cleared his throat. "Who is Claus Laufenburg?" he read.

There was a wide silence.

"Is that it?" asked Newman from the side.

"Oh," said Crispin, "no." He cleared his throat again. "Who is John Worley?" he read.

"Is that relevant?" asked Newman.

"Yes. Maybe. John Worley is the only person I asked who didn't know of Claus. It must mean something."

Newman came over, took the book from his hands and flipped through its pages. When he saw it was empty apart from the two questions, he returned it to Crispin, beckoned to Marc Almond, took a folder from the latter and, riffling through the pages within, eventually found what he was looking for. This he put into Crispin's hands, instructing him to read. It was a print-out of the e-mail Crispin had first written to Newman. Crispin quailed somewhat knowing he would have to read the names of so many of those present. It was as if he were about to perform a striptease with no practice. Yet, he reflected fleetingly, this was precisely the moment of shame, nakedness and release a writer seeks, wanting the precariously maintained double-triple-quadruple-life finally to fall to pieces and end.

"Dear Kim Newman," he began, "I am writing to you with information related to an undefined something, which I hardly know how to name at the beginning of this e-mail, since the name Claus Laufenburg is merely a reference point for something that requires some other name in order to be understood. I hope that you might be able to help me in defining this something, naming this other name. It was you I thought of when this matter brought me to my state of current perplexity, since no other person of whom I know better fits the description 'one-man panopticon of the weird'. . ."

And he continued to read, without hurrying, the entire e-mail. People, he realized, were listening. He was tempted to smirk at the worst of his phrases, to signal his own distance from himself, but when he dared steal glances at the assembled he saw that they were attentive, receiving the living information with seriousness and sensitivity—there was simply no need for anyone to smirk at the verbal squirmings that were nothing more than the wave pattern particular to the truth all understood was now unfolding.

At last he came to the end. There was hesitant clapping. Was this the kind of thing one clapped? It was hard to know. Nonetheless, after initial uncertainty, the clapping caught on and attained respectable volume. Newman thanked Crispin and took the microphone once more.

Upon the ground laid by Crispin, who descended once more to the audience, Newman proceeded to work. The process was disorganized but energetic. Newman called up witnesses and quizzed them on their various relationships with Claus Laufenburg. Had they met him in person? Where? What had he spoken about? Had he given any biographical details? Was he alone or accompanied? And so on. Anything that seemed significant, or that tallied with or contradicted the testimony of another witness, was noted down in a document by Marc

Almond, who now sat a few feet away from Newman at a desk with a laptop.

Very soon patterns began to emerge and some curious phenomena were apparent in the accumulating data. First of all, although it was true that some of the assembled had met Claus Laufenburg, he had never been accompanied, had always chosen, himself, the time and place of the meeting, and had, it seemed, unobtrusively choreographed all important factors. For instance, it was notable that no two people in the room had seen Claus Laufenburg at the same time, although there were many people here who socialized together. But far more striking facts than this soon took shape when the knowledge of one person was correlated with the knowledge of another. Someone told of how they had received from Claus the touching gift of the handwritten diaries of John Balance from Coil, covering the years 1995 to 1998, and immediately it was discovered that someone else present had given those same diaries to Claus as a token of appreciation four years before the first witness had received them. When this came to light, Newman, sensing a lead, immediately focused the questioning on gifts received from or made to Claus. This proved a rich seam to mine. David Ryder Prangley had given Claus an initialed knuckleduster, which he had later passed on to Simone Salvatori. Lisa Gerrard had received from him a signed publicity still of Tura Santana, only to learn that Claus himself had received it from Justin Isis. In some cases, Claus had given the same gift to more than one person after it had returned to him from other hands than those he had previously passed it into. An Amazonian blowpipe with darts, which had reputedly once been the property of William S. Burroughs, was found to have passed through the hands of five of those present. Or rather, it remained in the hands of one of these five. Claus had given it to three of these, two of these had given it to two of the others, and these two had given it to Claus. None had known of this chain until this evening. One or two chains were even longer, including the chain that involved a pair of leg warmers once worn by Kate Bush.

So widespread and peculiar was this circulation of gifts that the question was raised as to what the motive of Claus might be in perpetuating it. However, no one mentioned his ever calling in onerous favors for himself or seeking objects without payment. Usually the favors he did seek were on behalf of others. Many claimed that simply by directing the right pair of eyes or ears in the right direction, he had facilitated the upward movement of their career. And the objects he sought were usually the creative products of the individual in question, paid for with good coin, and since none could remember actually buying from him, it was hard to suppose he was selling such items at profit.

What did he do, then, in other life, to earn the coin he spent? This question returned attention to the mystery of the many addresses of Claus Laufenburg. Of one person he would request that they send a signed book—because of complications with his home address—to his place of work, which happened to be a morgue in Düsseldorf. To another, giving a similar reason, he would supply the address of a contraband storage facility in Lima, Peru. He worked apparently in an astronomical observatory—

if these addresses could be trusted—and as a breeder of champion pigeons. It was not that he never used the same address twice, but it was surely clear that no human could work so many jobs at such geographical distances from each other without the quality of their work suffering to an unacceptable degree.

What could it portend?

As the atmosphere became increasingly lively, restraint fell away from those gathered and here and there, when individuals were given more time to speak, there emerged some truly outré anecdotes. To relate them all would be to step beyond the limits of this tale; the following, therefore, must stand as representative of them all. It was told by the recently favored comic book writer, Alan Moore.

Alan had, it seems, been strolling along Garrick Street on a dark and chill October evening when he recognized a figure on the pavement ahead, whom he proceeded to trail. This figure—Claus Laufenburg, he was sure, by the inimitable gait and silhouette—stopped for a moment outside one of the famous secondhand bookshops near Cecil Court, glanced in the window, and stepped within. Alan, thinking it were a merry thing to combine a chance meeting with a secondhand bookshop, followed. He entered in time to see Claus deposit a very large, leather-bound book with the clerk in the far corner before descending the stairs to the basement, where more books were stored. Alan descended after him, but, to his astonishment, found the narrow, book-crammed basement empty of any human presence but his own. Somewhat unnerved, he checked again the alcoves to each side. As he was doing so, he noticed a flickering light seemingly coming from behind the books at the basement's far end. Thinking there might be a hidden room, he rushed over and removed the books between which the light had been flickering. The light, however, disappeared, and all that was uncovered was the wall behind the bookcase. Puzzled and disoriented, Alan blundered out of the shop, looking for, but not finding, Claus. Once outside on the street again, he looked up at the sky to see a curious thing. The blackest of clouds above was flickering with a yellow light like a faulty electrical fitting, its rhythm exactly like that of the mysterious light he had seen in the basement. There was no murmur of thunder, however. Alan was mesmerized. The evening took on a strange and puzzling warmth, as of some nameless benevolence.

The next week, when he was home once more in Nottingham, Alan received an unexpected brown-paper parcel. Inside was a first edition of Denton Welch's *A Voice Through a Cloud*, bearing the stamp of the book-shop he had visited in London. The note was from Claus and read, "It was lovely to see you in London the other day. Sorry I had no time to stop and talk."

Voices, in the Horse Hospital, became louder, more excited. It was hard to keep the room quiet enough for any length of time for individuals to be heard out. Moreover, rather than provide an answer for the question with which the evening had started, the meeting of those related through Claus Laufenburg and the sharing of tes-timonies seemed only to have added mystery to mystery.

"But how," someone was saying, "could Claus Laufenburg have met you in Kuala Lumpur at five o'clock

that day and me in Milan at eight o'clock? Time differ-
ence? Oh . . ."

"What about John Worley?" someone else was shouting from near the back.

Kim Newman was still at the microphone on the
stage. "I fear we're getting off track." He spoke like a
Canute attempting to command a tide of noise.

It was ten minutes or so since Alan Moore had given
his testimony and descended, once more, to the crowd.
Crispin stood still, brooding, his ears numbed by the
din. He looked around and a curious, sickening thought
came to his mind. If a ship in a storm, he reflected,
was approaching a jagged rock, if the wheel had been
abandoned and all passengers and crew were engaged in
squabbles, and if then one person saw the unattended
wheel and the jagged rocks and was awake to the situation, that person could not, with easy conscience, use the
fact that no one else thought to take the wheel to absolve
himself for not taking it.

He made his way once more through the crowd to the
stage, stepped up at the side and approached the microphone. Newman looked at him sidelong as he drew near.
He was searching for words, not sure how to ask now for
what had been given before, but there must have been
something in his expression because Newman yielded his
place to him before he made a sound. This acquiescence,
in turn, had a quietening influence on the room; though
there were still voices raised, Crispin saw that the attention directed at him would spread if he addressed it. He
stood for a moment before the microphone, meditating
his words. Then he spoke:

"I think . . ." More voices dropped away. "I am beginning to think we are prying into things of which it is better to remain ignorant. What do we think we will find out? How do we think we will benefit from it? I know I started this, but . . . I feel as if the skin containing us is wearing thin, and might burst, and what matters most is just that the skin carries us. We are known to each other and to Claus. Maybe that's as far as it should go. I'm sure it's a good thing not to take this for granted, but when we question it too much . . . I remember the words now of Frankie Howerd when he gained a younger audience towards the end of his life. 'You must never question it,' he said. Maybe one last question: Has anyone here suffered misfortune as a result of knowing Claus?"

At last there was complete silence.

"Then," said Crispin, "I suggest we keep this matter only in our hearts, and adjourn."

Nearly a week had passed since Crispin's speech had brought a strange, sudden autumn to that room, so that those assembled were, soon thereafter, scattered like leaves. He had done little in the meantime except read over his published works and his old e-mails to friends and acquaintances. The former he had written, always, in the hope that each might somehow be able to stand alone for the whole of his life; the latter he had written as the occasion demanded, often enough to settle the urge of a moment. Yet he found that there was seldom as much of his true vitality in his published works as there was in his off-hand e-mails. And since both published works and e-mails would no doubt be lost and forgotten, he wondered why he had gone so very much out of his way, at least for the former.

His way. But then, he reminded himself, it was not really out of but in his way that he had gone, however "out of" it seemed from a worldly point of view. *In* his dratted way—that was the trouble. There was some kind of contradiction here, he noticed, but he had never solved it before and was not likely to now.

It was in the conditions of lease that he should not smoke in his flat, and, indeed, he rarely did so, but now he was sitting in his armchair with a cigarette in one hand and an ashtray in the other, and only the kitchen window open to mitigate the delinquency. There seemed little reason to care about anything, and sadly still less reason to make any extravagant gesture of daring. His speech had been . . . a kind of triumph, that was true. Although "triumph" was the wrong word. It was not that it had been his finest hour in any sense that might imply trophies and honors—no, it had merely been his truest hour. And what remained for him now that it had passed? He was not a good enough writer to tackle the titanic moral issues that stacked up on the world's horizon. He was not good enough to capture the depths of two different souls in order even to differentiate one character from the next. And yet he saw what towered on the horizon and what glistened in the waters of the living souls around him. He was helpless. Fate had conferred on him the role of bad entertainer, and he must accept it with as little display as possible of his anguish and self-disgust, except, of course, insofar as those things, too, were bad entertainment.

He supposed that sooner or later he would even have
to start writing again.

Something like shame had forced him out of his usual
needy routine of checking the internet for messages, but,
as he finished his cigarette and realized he did not feel like
reading a book, he decided to log on and see what flickers
of pseudo-life there might be in the digital glade.

He went first to his e-mail in-box and found there a
single unread message. It was from Claus Laufenburg,
under the subject heading, "Splendidly cerebral sep-
puku." He had not heard from Claus, he reflected, since
the day he had attended the Momus gig. He thought of
all that had happened in the intervening days, so much
of it concerning the author of this as yet unread e-mail.
Why, he wondered, had he been in such a funk since
the meeting at the Horse Hospital? After all . . . after
all . . . no one was equipped to understand his own life
like he did, and here he was, against incalculable odds,
at its very center, and about to click on an e-mail from
Claus Laufenburg. He felt as if he were floating in a
coruscating soap bubble.

The e-mail read:

> Dear Crispin,
>
> I hope recent events in your life are to
> your satisfaction.
>
> It would be karmically suitable were that
> to be the case, since I have been reading,
> while you have been going about your per-
> sonal business, *The Ritual Disembowelment
> of My Sick Mind*, and finding it very satisfy-

ing indeed. I am undecided as to which I enjoy more—your fabulous fictions or those pieces that seem—though I dare not pry in this matter—somewhat in the nature of autobiographical essays. But since I am happy to be thus suspended in a state of indecision between ample pleasures, I see no reason to decide, and will only say that you do both marvelously.

Alas, I know only too well that such writing will likely only receive wider recognition after the tragic, and possibly agonizing, death of the author in question, if ever, but I for one would be astonishingly pleased if you were to continue to bear this burden, and write—as if nothing else mattered.

Well, I do hope we will have another chance to meet sometime.

If there is anything at all I can do for you, let me know.

Yours in a not-to-be-ignored spirit of
affirmation,
Claus.

Crispin leaned back in his chair, his hand to his mouth as if searching for a missing moustache, and mused.

"Anything at all?"

The letters of those two short, abstract words, "at all," grew, as he pondered them, into towering monuments constructed of stone blocks so massive it was a riddle how they were lifted one atop another.

Beyond these sky-challenging letters there became visible, as if curtains of primaeval mist had by fairy hand been drawn aside, a sun-anointed landscape where ferns and mosses like delicate sea anemones, not only green, but tinted in roseate pink and in gold and blue, made rich the shelter lent by coral reefs of trees, these, in turn, crowning and girding hills anciently virgin in their expressive glow of spiritualized nature, like the hills of a painting by Fra Angelico. And in a dew-enlivened gulley between two such hills, where winsome jellyfish frisked upon the limpid air like dragonflies, there sat in a circle of communion some dozen or so human souls—embodied or not it was difficult, perhaps even irrelevant, to say—each adorned with paints and fabrics and stitches of brocade that bespoke the art of wise and happy fingers, and all together—with the frolicking of their painted, unclothed offspring in the sponge-deep moss nearby—exemplifying what great fulfilling peace at last had resulted from the dreadful crucible of human history. One among them—Crispin, immersed in this vision, now saw—had his face, the lines of anxiety and pettiness melted from it to release the bright livingness he believed it once had rayed before, long ago. This other self, somehow resurrected here, in a future paradise, moved his lips and spoke, and though there were none of the hesitations and calculations, the blots and revisions, to which he was accustomed in preparing the written word, the syllables of speech flew gentle and perfect from that other tongue as if each word were a downy dandelion seed whisked by a breeze. In fact, as he watched, the word-seeds alighted in the landscape here and there and new delights sprouted and blossomed in each place. Having spoken, the man—this other Crispin—stood, nobly semi-naked, and proceeded over the blissful rug of herbage to a great, pink tree trunk, hollow-branched, like sky-seeking lightning from the earth, and he entered within and raised his voice again, and in the echoes that blew through each branch as through a sounding horn, he heard the joyous eternity of those already gone beneath the soil . . .

With the vision still firm upon its foundation of cloud before him, Crispin clicked "Reply." But what could he write? Could he dare to ask?

He sobbed and turned away from the screen.

"But you've given me so much already."

He would prepare an answer later, when the clouds, having rained, had let go the burden of the vision. He would think of something appropriate—hesitating, calculating. For now, he knew, he must lie down.

Damian Murphy

One Thousand Sleeping Souls
Lie Best
Unknowing and Distressed

EVERY evening as his shift began, Claus would take himself directly to one of the offices in the north-eastern quarter of the complex. There, he would switch on the transistor radio that sat upon a wooden ledge above a cabinet. He would carefully tune the dial to a space just on the edge of a legitimate station, evoking a sea of static in which only the faintest traces of distorted speech or music could be discerned. The volume was turned to its lowest possible setting, just enough to penetrate the silence. The transmission would proceed to permeate the atmosphere like a subtle and insidious intoxicant, drifting out through the open door and contaminating the reaches beyond.

Claus had arrived a couple of minutes late, as was his habit. He lost no time at all in proceeding to the office in question. Once he'd adjusted the lighting to create a desirable aesthetic and set the transmissions of the radio to his satisfaction, he sat himself in the welcoming embrace of the armchair before the main work desk. The blotter before him was littered with log books and papers, the latter invariably dated, signed, and initialed in glistening black ink. He let himself relax for several seconds, taking in the pleasing arrangement of furniture and décor. Several unconnected objects vied for his attention: a rosewood divan with silken upholstery, a framed reproduction of an etching of the Tempio di Stafano Rotondo, a bust of Goethe that perched like an agnostic angel between two rows of hardbound books on one of the shelves. He felt as much at home in the other man's workspace as he did in his own apartment.

Claus had spent the better part of the past week slowly mastering the handwriting of the man that worked in the office by day. He'd exerted an admirable degree of effort in the imitation of his signature—its extravagant loops and flourishes having clearly been developed over many years of arduous and self-conscious practice. Opening one of the heavy drawers, he retrieved a sheet of official letterhead, cleared a space before him on the blotter, and uncapped one of the pens. He let his mind go perfectly blank, drew his breath into the cavern of his chest, lowered his head, put pen to paper, and began to compose:

> Dear sirs, madams, gentle people of the laity, and God's involuntary martyrs,
>
> Mark well upon your consciences the wails of the perplexed lest your souls be spared the insidious trials to come.
>
> Regress! Resound! Resume! Undress! One thousand sleeping souls lie best unknowing and distressed.

Let your wives be given over to the ordeals of the vexed, your husbands stripped of dignity in the wake of their transgressions, your sons and daughters ill-conceived in the abysses of contention and your ancestors forgotten in their excess—for thus, and only thus, might the toil of your loins forsake the fruit of their aberrant ministrations.

Let us also not forget the degradations of the text.

My fellows, my colleagues, my asparagus, my flesh, I implore you in the very name of GOD,

Gottlieb Köhl

The sheet was neatly folded three times by Claus's culpable fingers, taken down the hall and around the corner to the marble-tiled receptionist room, and dropped, beneath the glow of the resplendent chandelier, into a brass slot marked "incoming" before it was altogether forgotten.

He returned to the office, settled back into the chair, and helped himself to a pouch of tobacco, rolling papers, and a box of matches found in one of the drawers. Within the space of a minute, the first rich burst of pungent smoke had filled his mouth. His customary cigarette comprised an illicit liberty that was far more addictive than the tobacco itself. The furtive act made him feel as if he had assumed the throne of a monarch *in absentia*.

With his cigarette in hand, he idly flipped through the pages of one of several wide booklets before him.

He took a cursory interest in the contents of the grids that stretched from one margin to the other. Debits, credits, balances, and dates sat next to license numbers, tide tables, and notes on the phases and houses of the moon. Other pages were entirely given to memorandums scrawled right over the top of the rows and columns. Among them, he found one of his own, a phrase that he'd surreptitiously added to the log book several weeks before: *Pity me! Succor me! Take me to the Temple!* He idly wondered if his work had been noticed.

Proceeding toward the end of the book, he found several tables which had not yet been filled out or written over. He took a few minutes to finish his cigarette in quiet contemplation. Over the course of several weeks, he had been slowly composing the elements of a brief narrative as he walked to and from his place of work. Casting the remains of his cigarette into an ornate, gold spittoon, he retrieved the pen with which he'd written his memo and set his story down in lines of stark, black ink.

A Flip-Take[1] in the Heart of Seville
by Leopold Nacht

". . . you should have seen the size of his monocle!" quipped Estrella, her glass of rosé reflecting the light of the torches that flamed like cardinals in flight above their heads.

———————————

1 Flip-take: an early comic strip trope in which the delivery of an unexpected rejoinder inspires the recipient to launch themselves backwards with a cloud of dust at their feet.

In response, Gustavo launched himself directly up and backwards as if whipped off his feet by a violent gale. He sailed right over the heads of the congregation and onto the trays of crème caramel that had been so thoughtfully arranged upon the tablecloth of Belgian lace. Gaspar eyed the ruinous display with unconcealed admiration. He quickly determined to top his rival's efforts with a flip-take of his own.

One day followed another with little incident. The situation in Morocco became increasingly delicate. A proclamation was made to the Berber tribes declaring Spanish soldiers unfit for the delights of Paradise. King Alfonso himself sent a telegram extolling the virtues of real men. Gaspar, meanwhile, kept himself occupied with the formulation of his plan.

One fine evening, as Gustavo passed from the brightly lit interior of El Rinconcillo into the moody embrace of the Calle Gerona, he was delighted to find his friend and associate awaiting him by the curbside. Gaspar was dressed in his most elegant finery and was accompanied by an unfamiliar woman. The two of them appeared to be involved in a fiery debate.

". . . a virgin devoured is never deflowered!" the woman declared just as Gustavo was about to greet them. Gaspar, feigning shock, jumped back with such unholy vehemence that he smashed right through the nearby window and sailed over several tables. The patrons inside gazed in baffled dismay as he collided with the shelves behind the bar. The catastrophe upset several rows of neatly lined-up bottles, bringing them crashing to the floor in an extravagant display of shattered glass and ruined spirits. The perpetrator of the accident was not entirely unharmed. Aside from sustaining several cuts and gashes on his arms and back, he'd managed both to break his wrists and dislocate a finger. Despite his obvious discomfort, he glowed with satisfaction like a clergyman engulfed in flame.

"The gesture is hardly genuine in any case," so Gustavo was heard to observe from outside. "One must never perform such a perilous act with the intention of doing so. A flip-take is bestowed as a grievous sacrament directly from the hands of the Holy One. Otherwise it's little more than a cheap diversion."

When he was released from the hospital, Gaspar privately settled his debt with the proprietor of El Rinconcillo. The following weeks found him conspicuously absent from the streets and public houses of Seville. Rumors passed among the daughters of the gentry like a flock of sparrows. It was whispered that he'd gone to a school in Bhutan to study with a venerated master of the art of the flip-take.

While Gaspar was away, the Moroccan conundrum continued to grow more dire. The blazing sun was relentless in its continual assault upon the soldiers in their makeshift barracks. A message was sent by heliograph from the Spanish garrison at Igueriben. It seemed the men encamped at the isolated fortress had been reduced to drinking ink. Gustavo, in the meantime, suffered a series of tumbles that scandalized his heritage and brought ignominy to his name.

With each act of disgrace, his infamy increased. His mishaps swiftly became legendary. A collection of priceless antiques was reduced to rubble at a séance on the outskirts of Santa Catalina; several notable dignitaries were crushed by falling masonry at a meeting among royalists in a secret chamber of the Alcázar; a brothel run illegally beneath the Torre del Oro became the site of a nationwide emergency—every flip-take outdid all of its predecessors by an order of magnitude. The population of Seville was made to tremble in anticipation of Gustavo's next outrageous leap. Finally, the reign of terror unexpectedly ceased, though many remained apprehensive that it was merely the calm before the storm.

A collective sigh was heard across the city as Gaspar was spotted on the streets once again. He was hailed by some as a holy savior, come to stop the madness that had plagued their institutions. Others revered him as an avenging angel that had struck the root of affliction from the heart of the city. Gustavo, however, feared the worst. He paid a visit to his former friend as soon as opportunity allowed him.

"I implore you," he pleaded. "Let us stop this inane competition. Too much is at stake. Too much of genuine value stands to be lost. The flip-take is not a sacrament, but the blight of a malicious star. It is the unalterable conclusion of a reign of iniquity which has collectively undermined our faith in God."

"How can you speak of such frivolous things at a time like this?" replied Gaspar, exasperated. "Forget your childish vanities! The Spanish army has failed us! Thousands lie dead at Annual, and countless more have gone missing on the outskirts of Melilla. General Fernández Silvestre has completely lost his mind and has taken to raving about the advance of the 'boogeyman' and order- ing his men to flee. Our efforts in North Africa have made us the laughingstock of all of Europe. The seeds of revolt have been sown among a restless and unstable populace, and here you are obsessed with children's games!"

The flip-take that followed made all that had come before it look negligible in comparison. Basilicas crumbled, the elect were unseated, and the monarchy itself was irrevocably undermined. The resulting mutiny among Spanish soldiers in Morocco preceded a military coup. The shadow cast over the face of Spain reached all the way to the crown. By the time it lifted, King Alfonso had renounced his throne. His remaining days were spent as a wandering exile, dispensing oracles and benedictions to the few remaining loyalists that were fortunate enough to cross his path.

Satisfied with the fruits of his whim, Claus carefully ripped the pages he'd defiled from their flimsily glued bindings. He placed them, face-up, on one side of the desk atop a disordered array of memorandums and reports. There he sat for several minutes, gazing mindlessly at Goethe's likeness on the far side of the room. The face of the poet was slightly turned to one side, his woeful expression bespeaking a dismay afforded only to the canonized. Claus rose from the chair, placed his palms together before him, briefly wondered where, within the boundaries of the complex, he might conceal his minor masterpiece, and headed out through the office door without bothering to close it behind him.

He proceeded down a corridor and through a heavy door into an ornate washroom. He was discouraged from using the facilities at night, save for the one reserved for employees of his rank located near the building's entrance. Though he'd been admonished for doing so on more than one occasion, he was hardly inclined to let this stop him. So far as he was concerned, the building belonged to him alone.

After dutifully fulfilling his biological needs, Claus stepped over to the sink and gazed at his reflection in the mirror. The image gazed back at him with unaffected disregard. He opened his mouth and swiftly closed it again, his jaw chomping down with mechanical precision. He shifted his eyes first to the left, then to the right, assuring himself that everything was still in proper working order. A moment of silence passed between the man and his reflection, broken only, at length, by a single syllable: "Claus."

The gesture was repeated without the slightest intention. It had never occurred to him how empty, yet how perfect, was the sound of his own name. "Claus," he said again, with no trace of inflection, fascinated by the way in which the word emitted from his lips. "Claus. Claus. Claus-claus. Claus. Claus-claus. Claus-claus. Claus-claus-claus."

Within a couple of minutes, the sound of the word had lost all trace of meaning. Further, it was difficult to discern where one "Claus" ended and the next began. He considered persisting for several hours, having little else of pressing interest with which to occupy himself. He chose, instead, to proceed directly to the next phase of the operation.

"Jonas," he uttered, with a sly, yet gentle insistence, a single eyebrow raised. The second name was so different from the first, being broken up in two parts. He repeated the experiment several times, allowing for subtle variations in enunciation. The sound of the syllables inordinately pleased him. "Jonas. Yoh. Nes. Nes-yoh. Jonas. Yoh-yoh. Nes-nes. Yooooooooooh-nes! Jonas-jonas. Jonas."

The sound of running water could be heard through the pipes. He wondered if he was not the only person in the building. Few worked at night. He enjoyed his hours of solitude above all else. His gaze shifted downward to a wooden plaque that leaned against the mirror on one side. Upon its face was found a set of instructions for the washing of the hands. The necessary steps were given in great detail, lest the critical procedure go awry:

> 1. Use soap and running water.
> 2. Rub your hands and arms vigorously for 20 seconds.
> 3. Wash all surfaces, including back of hands, wrists, between fingers, and under fingernails with a fingernail brush. Rinse your hands well.
> 4. Dry your hands with a paper towel.

Claus was left unsatisfied by the instructions. He felt as if the message was not at all as it ought to be. It lacked the perplexing whimsicality that even the most trivial of items should possess. He convinced himself that it was a matter of duty to address the deficiency.

He stepped out of the washroom and passed through the first door on his left, traversing a labyrinth of narrow corridors with steadfast determination. He passed through meeting rooms hung with lamps encased in domes of crystal. High windows with delicate arches gave view to auxiliary chambers crammed with archaic memorabilia. The lights of flaming candelabras revealed statuettes arranged like fetishes, their stoic glances trained on richly jeweled knives and unfolded paper fans. One chamber led to another, each of them housing a series of logbooks with index numbers stamped in gold upon their spines. Long shadows flickered like fleeing doves on the surfaces of polished meeting tables. At last, after nearly a quarter of an hours' search, Claus stumbled upon a storage space that was sure to contain the sought-after item.

Returning to the washroom with a piece of chalk in hand, he proceeded to flip the plaque over, its face now lying on the counter. Upon its unmarked back, he inscribed a proper set of instructions that left little room for ambiguity.

1. Wash hands, wrists, ankles, and snout.
2. Apply the Oxford comma.
3. Pernoctate for several minutes. Burst the bonds of double water. Count to six on soapy ring fingers. Stifle as appropriate.
4. Feel pleasant. Feel perplexed. Feel appropriate. Don't feel at all.
0. (Addendum) Count the seconds remaining to countdown. If zero, re-apply.

Satisfied with his redress, he tossed the chalk into the waste bin and leaned the plaque up in reverse against the mirror. Upon returning to his favorite office, he was dismayed to find that he'd forgotten all about the matter of what to do with the pages he'd ripped from the logbook. The problem genuinely vexed him. As important as the act of writing was, it paled in comparison to what was to be done with the completed text. He'd initially planned to hide the pages, stashing them perhaps inside the ventilation system, yet upon reflection he felt this wasn't quite enough.

He returned to his place behind the desk and spent several minutes wrapped in contemplation. Just as he was reaching for a second cigarette, he was graced with an epiphany. He raised his eyes to the bust of Goethe. The natural philosopher looked back at him with unambiguous disdain. Never before had the illustrious figure appeared so dignified in his eyes. He was tempted to kiss his white marble temples, to taste the minerality of his solemn brow, to press his nostrils against the veins of his neck that he might inhale the salt of his genius. Rising from the chair, he gathered the logbook pages in his hands and proceeded to the shelf that housed the statue. The chunk of sculpted stone was significantly heavier than he'd expected. Supporting it with both his arms as it leaned against his chest, he proceeded beneath the shadow of the door frame and out beneath the scintillating lamps that illuminated the corridor.

The author and statesman looked far from pleased as they passed by stained wooden panels and jeweled escritoires. His eyes, as smooth and white as eggs, gazed up imploringly as if to appeal to Claus's better nature. The latter was a temple of unfettered desire, his heart untouched by doubt or trepidation. He slipped through a doorway and marched up a winding stairway, the weight of the marble steadily increasing as he ascended toward the rooftop. When at last he breached the final door and emerged beneath the naked starlight, his burden felt no heavier than a discarded memorandum.

A soft cascade of fine, white mist was descending from the heavens. Claus relished the sensation of the rain on his face. Within seconds, his beard was inundated and his shirt nearly soaked through. He took the items in his arms to a stone balustrade that lined one edge of the rooftop, set them down on the flat expanse of tar, and placed one foot upon the pages so that they wouldn't fall prey to the caprices of the wind. Already, the paper was soaking up the rain. The ink had begun, almost imperceptibly, to run down the surface of the uppermost page. A glance over the edge revealed a nighttime street as desolate as a church. Satisfied that he wasn't putting anyone in physical danger, he lifted the marble bust with both his hands and hefted it up against his chest. With a strenuous lunge that sent a bolt of pain through his lower back, he tossed it, without a trace of remorse, over the edge.

The philosopher's likeness sailed seven stories down like an anchor dropped from Heaven, shattering at last into innumerable pieces on the cold, hard pavement below. So far as he knew, the impact was witnessed only by the streetlamps. The shards looked like a smear of crystal, the occasional jagged edge presenting a minor hazard to passing motorists. He was tempted to take the pages back down to the office, spoiled as they were, and leave them in the vacant space from which the bust had been taken. He decided instead to stick to his original plan. One after another were they tossed over the edge, listlessly sailing in lazy spirals to the unwashed surface of the street. Four of them could be seen lying on their backs like invalids among the scattered shards of marble; the others were entirely lost.

Claus remained perched on the rooftop for a little while longer, his body impervious to the soft assault of the elements. The night surged through him like a sinuous flame, its desolate caresses ennobling his heart with a virtue that was far from certain. He wondered what manner of signal was playing on the radio down below. Like an oracle, it never ceased to emit, never failed to cauterize the nightly wound he opened with his frivolous activities. Word of his transgression couldn't fail to get back to the agency. It was unlikely that they'd terminate his contract, yet he felt it best to prepare for the worst. He was ready to accept the consequences of his act, whatever they might be. In any case, they could hardly prevent him from gaining access to the building. He had various means at his disposal of finding his way into the interior. There were little-known doors and architectural aberrations, along with other, more subtle portals. He was a craftsman in the true sense, a dissenter and a master thief, and his desires would be thwarted by no one.

James Champagne

Dreamachine

DESPITE the fact I've been staying at this resort for over a month now, I still haven't been able to shake the feeling of dislocation that overcomes me when I first wake up. Every morning when I open my eyes I expect to see the familiar details of my apartment: the Madonna, Duran Duran, and Culture Club rock posters, the framed Patrick Nagel and Herb Ritts art prints, the Austin Osman Spare illustration of a satyr with an erection, the neon trim lighting and the furniture done in muted pastels. Instead I see a room with heavy drape curtains on the windows, expensive-looking rugs with florid Middle-Eastern designs, and it's like, "Who has warped me back to the Middle Ages?" Gradually I come to the realization that I am *not* back in my apartment in Room 23 of the Salome Heights building on Ocean Drive in South Beach, Miami. Rather, I am in my villa at the Qasr Al Wahum (which, in English, roughly translates to "Illusion Palace"), a 5-star resort located on the northeast border (near the Liwa Oasis) of the Rub' al Khali desert, otherwise known as "The Empty Quarter."

I get out of bed, carefully make it, then walk over to the terrace of my room and step outside, into the sweltering morning sun, completely naked. From my vantage point up here I have a great view of Qasr Al Wahum. Spread out over 19,000 acres and rising out of the desert like a shimmering hallucination, the resort (true to its name) resembles a fortress, only the type of fortress one can only see in fever dreams: everywhere I look I can see turrets, crenellated walls, mock-battlements, bubbling fountains and heavy, studded mahogany doors, all done in an Islamic style. The resort boasts 158 rooms (42 of which are multi-bedroom villas with their own terraces: I myself am staying in one of these rooms), and offers such luxuries as a pool, various restaurants, a gift shop, and a disco, plus activities like archery, yoga, tennis, horseback riding, dune walks, land sailing, and falconry. And yet despite all this activity it's the silence of the desert that surrounds me on all sides that gets to me. The heat I can deal with; after all, I've been living in Miami now for around 9 months. But that silence . . . luckily I made sure to bring my Sony Walkman with me.

Looking out at the desert, I think back to the events that led to me coming out here in the first place, but it's all kind of hazy. My band, Timewave Zero, had been doing a concert at Madison Square Garden to support our just-released debut album *2012* when I had a very public meltdown and fled the venue halfway through the show. Then I spent some time running around Times Square, where I saw a wall of TVs display an image of Vanna White turning around letter tiles on *Wheel of Fortune* to reveal the word ESCHATON. Then I flew back to

Miami and got shitfaced at Club Hell, where I watched a fake snuff film, listened to some Siouxsie & the Banshees, and got gang-raped by some punks (though is it rape if you enjoyed it? Or if you paid them a thousand dollars to do it? Anyway, I knew they didn't have AIDS because, despite being in a drunken state, I made sure to check their auras first).

Obviously a change in my life was needed, so I decided to just hop in a plane and abandon my old life. I first flew to a desert in Asia, the Gobi to be specific, which I wandered into after throwing away my portable phone, my Walkman, my wallet, my Mastercard, and so on: but then I did a reality check, scooped all that shit back up, and got the hell out of there (as if I could abandon my credit card!). I then took another plane to the United Arab Emirates, where I checked into the Qasr Al Sarab (under a fake name: Raoul Revere). Some people might think that's cheating, but what the hell, I'm still near a desert and it's dry and hot so, like, I think it counts? Anyway, the date is sometime in May, 1986, which means I've been out here for around 3 months now, though the concept of time out here seems very abstract and distant to me.

I turn away from the sight of the resort and step back into my villa. I walk into my bathroom, gaze at my reflection in one of the large mirrors that stretches from the floor to the ceiling. My name is Sypha Nadon. I'm 21 years old, though in terms of looks I can easily pass for 17 or 18. I have blond hair and blue eyes, pale and flawless skin (despite living in a desert for months now, I seem unable to get a tan), and I stand a little under six feet tall, being very thin as well. I am also extremely attractive, to the extent that just looking at my own reflection turns me on in a sexual manner. But I don't feel like jerking off right now so I just brush my teeth and slap on some clothes: today I'm wearing a red tank top with a Huw Feather design on the front (this displays the Psychic TV skull tattoo I have on my right shoulder: Marc Almond has a similar tattoo in this very spot). I also put on a pair of tight black jeans and shoes made of red leather. I then put on a pair of Wayfarer sunglasses and, on the way out of my suite, grab my Sony Walkman and some reading material. I head down to the lobby and go to the restaurant, where I have a breakfast that consists of camel milk and dates. I then leave the main hotel and make my way to the pool.

I'm resting on a lounge chair underneath an umbrella by the side of the resort's sprawling pool, which is surrounded by tall palm trees. The pool is quite busy this morning, and everywhere I look I can see beautiful tanned women with big tits in skimpy swimsuits cavorting with beautiful young tanned men with blond hair and . . . skimpy swimsuits. Like me, they're all wearing Wayfarer sunglasses. The sight isn't anything I haven't seen before (I can see people who look identical to these tourists everyday in South Beach just looking out my window, so the spectacle doesn't interest me too much). My attention wanders: I see people eating at Ghadeer (the poolside restaurant), resort employees using golf buggies to ferry around both the guests and their luggage, and, in the desert beyond the resort, I spot Demi Moore taking part in a Herb Ritts fashion shoot, which makes me flash back to the last time that Demi and I hung out, when we had lunch at Glasnost earlier this year. I remember for that lunch she was wearing a black skirt from Barney's and a turquoise Oscar De La Renta T-shirt. I turn my attention back to the pool and spot Dmitri, this hunky Russian bodybuilder who I hope to have sex with sometime soon. He waves to me and I smile and wave back. I then look down at the book in my lap that my guru, Claus, gave me to read: *The Spiritual Teaching of Ramana Maharshi*. I flip open to a random page and read an equally random sentence ("The Self is God") but then my eyes glaze over and I get bored so I put the book down and grab the May 1986 issue of *VOGUE* (the front cover model is Paulina Porizkova as photographed by Richard Avedon, with hair by Suga and makeup by François Nars). I have the head-phones of my Sony Walkman on and am listening to an ABBA cassette tape.

The song "Voulez-Vous" is playing and I'm glancing at a photospread of Cindy Crawford modeling a $52 Gottex string bikini when I notice, out of the corner of my eye, my guru, Claus Laufenburg, slinking out from behind the cover of a palm tree and walking in my direction. He's an older German guy (I think he's from Düsseldorf) with a bald head and a moustache. A few seconds later he's standing over me and staring down at my choice of reading material with disapproval. "Not exactly on the fast track to enlightenment, are we?" he asks, only a little sarcastically.

"Hey, I finished this book," I say, putting the *VOGUE* down and picking up the Ramana Maharshi book.

"Indeed? So then, could you provide me a synopsis of what the book's about? Encapsulate its main theme?" Claus asks, raising an eyebrow.

"Um, well, it's about, like . . . you know . . . uh . . . meditating and . . . Nirvana and self-realization and . . . meditating," I answer, somewhat lamely.

Claus rolls his eyes. "I think you're losing focus, Mr. Nadon," he says sternly. "I think we should have another session tonight. Perhaps after dinner, at my villa?"

"Yeah, sounds good," I say. "See you then."

Claus nods and walks off. I turn back to my copy of *VOGUE* and begin reading an article on Whitney Houston.

Later on in the day, after I finish my dinner (during the dinner, in the resort's main restaurant, I bumped into Fad Gadget, who told me that he had come to Qasr Al Wahum to take part in a commercial for Panasonic that was due to film in the desert the next day), I head up to Claus's villa, which is actually fairly close to my own. I first met Claus about a week or two after I arrived at the resort, and, quickly recognizing that I needed spiritual guidance, he took me under his wing. Since then I meet with him for private one-on-one sessions every couple of days, usually at night. Because he's older than me we don't have a lot in common, though some of our musical tastes match up: we're both fans of Soft Cell, Coil, Current 93, Throbbing Gristle, and so forth.

Not only is Claus's villa close to mine, it even looks pretty much identical, though he's personalized his a bit with little touches, such as Aubrey Beardsley art prints and lots of books, mainly texts dealing with Eastern religions, pretentious French Decadent writers like Jean Lorrain, and lots of horror and supernatural books. There is also a dreamachine spinning around in one corner of the room, casting eerie flickers of light along the walls of the darkened apartment. I have no idea if Claus created this dreamachine himself or if it's just something he picked up somewhere (maybe at Hammacher Schlemmer?), and I have no intention of asking him. When I arrive Claus is wearing an oriental-looking smoking jacket and bejeweled red slippers with curled toes, and atop his head, a black fez, which kind of startles me, though I should be used to it by now. After a formal greeting, he walks over to his stereo system and puts on a Chris & Cosey CD (*Trance*). He then takes a seat on a leather chair and I take a seat on an identical-looking chair across from him, so that we're facing each other. And then the session begins.

"The body has nine gates . . . it is the City of Nine Gates, though those of a Gothic persuasion might classify it as a Great Wound with Nine Openings," Claus says at one point in a hushed voice. In the background the song "The Gates of Ancient Cities" is playing, which strikes me as an odd coincidence.

"Um-hmm, yeah, I can dig that," I say, nodding my head, even though I have no idea what he is talking about, as usual.

"Tell me again what made you decide to come to the Empty Quarter?" he asks.

"I felt like I needed a change in my life," I sigh. "For months now I've been suffering from this lame nightmare where I saw myself wandering in a desert, and at the end of this desert was a mountain, which seemed to symbolize to me, like, an obstacle that needed to be overcome, you know? I feel as if there's a malignant emptiness inside me, and that I need to confront this emptiness, this abyss in my soul . . . so, a place called the Empty Quarter seemed like it would be the ideal battleground for such a confrontation to occur . . . you know?"

"That seems like a . . . strangely spiritual aspiration for you," Claus says, looking at me oddly.

"Hey man, I've always been . . . spiritual," I protest. "I'm a practicing chaos magician, I studied under Kenny Grant . . . hell, I once I dressed up like an alien butterfly for the Rite of Camazotz and gave a blowjob to a Mayan bat-squid god in a decrepit crypt in Wales."

"Oh Sypha, don't be so bourgeois, this is 1986, who *hasn't* done something like that these days?"

After the session, before we head our separate ways, Claus offers me a TaB diet cola soft drink, which I suppose is keeping things old school.

After leaving Claus's villa I head down to the resort's disco, which is located on the first floor of the main building, not that far from the primary restaurant. The disco is a large, shadowy room, the only lights coming from the dance floor area and the bar. There's a seating area near the bar, and a stage near the dance floor itself:

also in one corner of the room is an arcade, and though most of the games on display are antiquated there is at least one new one, *Rampage*, that I've played in the past. At the moment I'm in the seating area, sipping a drink while watching the people on the dance floor dance. On the stage there is one lone Arab boy in sloppy drag, who I guess is kind of cute, and he's dramatically lip-singing to the song currently blasting over the disco's speakers, which is "L'esqualita" by Soft Cell, off their underrated third album *This Last Night in Sodom*. Qasr Al Wahum's disco is nowhere near as exciting a place as, say, Club Wilde! back at SoBe but I suppose that there are worse places to spend one's evening. Right now I'm wearing a white The Police T-shirt, tight pants made of black leather, and, around my neck, a mauve-colored lightweight lace scarf tasseled with teardrop fringes.

I'm so distracted by the Arab boy in drag that I initially don't notice that Dmitri is by my table, trying to get my attention. He asks if I want to dance and, having nothing better to do, I say sure. So I follow him to the dance floor and we dance to Soft Cell. After the song he asks if I want to go back to his room. I'm tempted, and almost say yes, until I remember Mark, who I guess you could say is my boyfriend, my man, who's back home in Miami, patiently awaiting my return. He's the one who saved me from those punk rocker gang-rapists at Club Hell a few months back. Feeling a twinge of guilt, I politely decline, and while Dmitri is disappointed he understands and we go our separate ways. I leave a tip for the bartender and go over to the arcade where I spend a few minutes playing *Rampage* (as usual, I play as the

Lizzie character). I quit after the beating the sixth screen, leaving behind the ruins of Kalamazoo, Michigan. Back in my villa I put on Siouxsie & the Banshees' *Juju* album and jerk off while listening to "Arabian Knights." I think back to what just occurred down at the disco, earlier in the evening, and wonder if this is a sign that maybe I'm growing as a human being.

That night as I lay in bed I think about all the things I currently miss. I miss my apartment in Miami. I miss my voluminous compact disc collection. I miss my pet dog, Glinka (a Basset Hound who enjoys eating Campbell's Soup). I miss my BMW. I miss Veronica. Surprisingly, I miss my parents, both long dead, who I never even got along with (my father dropped dead from a fatal heart attack in 1977 when he and my mom came home early from a vacation and caught me rimming my 19 year-old brother in the shower . . . I was 13 at the time . . . my mother went insane and overdosed on marijuana a few months later, and the following year my brother killed himself). Most of all, I miss Mark. I miss his clean-cut All-American boy looks, the dimples of his friendly smile, the masculine smell of his aftershave, the way I feel safe when he holds me in those muscular arms of his.

A few days later Veronica Akita, my agent/best friend, drops by the resort to see how I'm doing. Contrary to what she's been telling others, she's the only other person I'm friends with who knows I'm up here. Right now we're in the resort's restaurant, having lunch, Arabic mezze.

Veronica is 22 years old, of Japanese origin (though her family moved to the USA when she was 15 and currently she lives in Miami), short and thin, a stunningly attractive woman with long brown hair, green/hazel eyes, and gigantic tits. Right now she's wearing a Venom T-shirt (on the front of the t-shirt is a black and white illustration of a goatish-looking demon face with an upside-down pentagram in between its eyes and the words "Black Metal" in Gothic lettering beneath this face) and a short skirt. Like me she's a graduate of UMASS, though she graduated a year before I did, being slightly older than me; it was actually at UMASS that we first met.

"So, how's the band doing?" I ask, as I take a sip of my camel milk. This morning I'm wearing a pink Izod Lacoste polo short-sleeved shirt (it has a little green reptile sewn onto the breast: I think it's supposed to be some species of dinosaur or maybe even a dragon) and very short denim shorts and on my feet I'm wearing huarache sandals.

"They're getting by," Veronica shrugs. "James is currently dating a female bodybuilder named Lauren . . . I think he may be undergoing a sex change as well. Oh, and he started writing a kid's book about a family of talking waffles. Bob is Bob: he actually married his fiancée recently . . . you've met her, Tina, you know, the Cat Band fan? Don't know what Hank is up to."

"Hank's an asshole," I sigh. "Still, I do feel bad missing Bob's wedding."

"I'm sure he understands," Veronica assures me in her girlish voice. She takes a sip of her camel milk hesitantly and makes a face. "So do you know when you're coming back yet?"

"I want to say next month, sometime in June, but it's still all up in the air," I admit.

It's later on in the afternoon and Veronica and I are out in the desert, practicing falconry. Joining us is the performance artist known as The Fabulous Mr. Meaningless, an old friend of mine who just so happened to be visiting the resort. The Fabulous Mr. Meaningless has the body of an enlarged dodo, white-gloved hands (but no apparent arms) jutting out of his feathery body, violins for legs, and atop a skinny neck his head consists of a giant eyeball (no nose, no ears, no mouth, no hair, just a giant fucking eyeball), and perched atop this eyeball is a black top hat tilted at a jaunty angle. He also wears a skinny black and white necktie done in a chessboard design. He lives out in East Corinth, a suburb in Cleveland, Ohio, in a gigantic house that, from the sky, resembles a large eyeball, thus completing the face of the architectural Jayne Mansfield. The last time I spoke with him we talked about the Crooked Universe and the new Madonna album and he juggled pumpkins and had a conversation with my shadow and he also mentioned something about assassinating the Pope. Anyway, it's good to see him again.

I gaze out at the desert surrounding us on all sides. The Rub' al Khali desert is the largest contiguous sand desert in the entire world, blanketing the southern third of the Arabian Peninsula . . . 250,000 square miles of sand dunes interspersed with gravel and gypsum plains, a wilderness larger than France. Due to feldspar, the sand here has a reddish-orange color, which is kind of cool, I guess. Here in this hyper-arid climate, the daily max temperature can hit 117 degrees Fahrenheit in July and August, but luckily today it's only in the upper 90s. Some fauna that may be found here in the Empty Quarter include scorpions, wild gazelles, snakes, sand foxes, camel spiders, assorted birds and rodents, oryxes, Saluki dogs, flamingos, and camels.

I turn my attention back to my friends. Veronica has changed into something a little more appropriate for the desert, a billowy white shirt that's very low-cut (exposing a large amount of cleavage) along with silk pants and sandals. One of the falcon handlers is alternately showing her how the falcons hunt their prey while also ogling at her boobs. Qasr Al Wahum is home to 9 falcons, of the peregrine/saker species, and when hunting prey these birds can attain speeds of 215 mph. Each bird has its own passport, which I think is pretty fab. The Fabulous Mr. Meaningless is fiddling around with a boom box, coasting through the channels until he finds a song he likes: he eventually settles on "Fall Into Glass" by E.G. Oblique Graph which is kind of conventional but okay, whatever. I'm reclining on some kind of desert lounge chair, lazily flipping through one of the books I brought along with me for the trip, a book I purchased at the airport, a book called *Being and Time* by some German guy and I think it's supposed to be some kind of murder mystery novel because I've read the first chapter and so far I have absolutely no idea what it's about. The three of us are just drifting . . .

The Fabulous Mr. Meaningless is telling me a joke (the punchline of which is, "Out of the next vineyard, where I saw a young deer hanging by his tail from a tree, as if someone had so punished him for stealing figs,") in his Fred Schneider voice and I'm just settling into a relaxed state of mind when I notice Claus step out from behind a sand dune. He's dressed in khakis and on his head is a pith helmet. "I see you're all on top of confronting that mountain, Sypha," he says with a smirk.

"Oh, I was just showing my friends the, you know, the falcons," I say as I put my book down next to me. "What's up?"

"I was thinking we should take a little ride out into the desert," Claus says. "There's something out there I need to show you."

"Can't it wait?" I groan. "I'm kind of mellowing out with my friends here, in case you, like, haven't noticed."

"You can 'mellow out' later, young man," Claus says sternly. "Let's get a move on, shall we?"

"Okay, okay," I grumble. "After all, you're the guru."

"How many times do I have to tell you, Sypha? I'm not the guru . . . the desert is," Claus sighs. He then walks off.

I explain to Veronica and the Fabulous Mr. Meaningless that I have an appointment to attend to, and that I'll see them later on at dinner. I then follow Claus. A few minutes later and we're on camels, riding out further into the desert. Claus is telling me how this desert served as the inspiration for Irem, the fictitious lizard-haunted City of

Pillars, but I'm barely paying attention. I'm thinking instead of all the other things I'd rather be doing right now: having brunch with Boy George, listening to "Angel" by Madonna over and over and over again, licking Mark's biceps, getting the high score on *Bubble Bobble*.

"This camel's name is Gimel, believe it or not," I eventually tell Claus, to break the silence, indicating the camel I'm on with a tilt of my head. "I think we've really bonded the last few months. He's only tried to hump me, like, five times. Have you ever been humped by a camel, man?"

"I can't say I have, no," Claus says, leading the way on his own camel. "Though when I was a child living on the North Sea, I was terrified of jellyfish."

"Far out," I say, wondering how that relates to my camel story. "And will you take off that grody pith helmet already? You look ridiculous."

"I don't want the top of my head to get sunburnt," Claus says through gritted teeth. "If you would just slather it with sunblock like I ask you to, it wouldn't be necessary."

"Hey, you can slather your own head, man," I say.

Eventually he brings us to a halt atop a sand dune and points to something in the distance. I look to where he's pointing and I can see, far into the desert, a towering mountain made of brown stone. "What do you think about that?" Claus asks me.

"It looks like an enormous dong," I say, lowering my Wayfarers.

"That, my young rapscallion, is the mountain from your dreams," Claus informs me. "I'm thinking we go out there, tonight, and climb to its summit. Don't worry; I've done this before . . . there's a pathway up so it's not a tough climb. Once we're at the top, then we can begin our final lesson. What do you say?"

"You're the boss," I say, because I can't think of anything else to say.

It's much later on in the evening and Claus and I have reached the summit of the mountain. I'm dressed much as I was earlier in the day, but Claus is now wearing an exotic-looking cymar with a Moroccan design (of all things). We're seated on a ledge overlooking the desert, and I must admit it's quite a pleasant sight. There's a full moon out, and the moonlight seems to make the sand of the Empty Quarter gleam. Lunar camels prowl the dunes, and in the far distance we can just make out the lights of the resort; from afar, it really does look like something right out of a Scherezadean fairy tale. Claus is droning on about something mystical and also mentions Atma Vichara (I think they're a band or something, might have seen them on MTV once but I'm not sure), but while he was talking I covertly slipped on the headphones of my Sony Walkman and right now I'm listening to "Desert Kisses" by Siouxsie & the Banshees, which seems to complement the imagery nicely.

Claus directs a question my way, and when I don't respond he looks over at me and notices the headphones. Sighing, he yanks them off. "This is no time for joking around, Sypha," he hisses. "Your moment of transcendence approaches!"

"What do you mean?" I ask. "Did you bring some coke with you?"

"I want you to look out at the desert and think of it as one enormous mirror."

"But I thought you said the desert was a guru," I point out, confused.

"The desert is a guru *and* a mirror," Claus helpfully clarifies. "Now, I want you to visualize the desert as a mirror that's reflecting your own image back at you. Tell me what that image is."

I look out at the desert before us and, after a few moments, say, "I see something that's . . . eternal. Unchanging. Something that has been here before my time and will still be here after I'm gone." I squint to be sure, then continue on to say, "I see the infinite."

"In that case, your mirror lies to you," Claus says. "Look more closely at those sand dunes down below. See how the wind is constantly shifting them, subtly changing their shapes, altering their nature. To see the desert as unchanging is an error, for the desert is *always* changing, always in a state of flux. Just as we ourselves are always in a state of flux. It just happens so slowly, so gradually, that we tend not to realize it. The bedrock upon which we build the scaffolding of our sense of Self is not made of stone, but rather sand. And thus our sense of Self is as utterly illusionary and transient as was your impression that the desert has always been and will always be one unchanging thing. The desert is a dreamachine, and

Chaos is the only constant. As a wise man once said, 'The price of existence is eternal warfare.'"

"Dude, so, like, what's your point?" I ask, a little disturbed by his soliloquy as I slip my headphones back on. "I came all the way out here to the middle of nowhere to prove to myself that I *wasn't* empty, and now you're telling me that the, uh, desert is telling me that's exactly what I am?"

"You came to a place called the Empty Quarter to find enlightenment . . . what did you expect?" Claus asks, raising an eyebrow (something he's been doing a lot of lately, I can't help but notice). "But do not despair. Though empty you may be, in your emptiness you're not alone, for I too am empty, as is your friend Veronica, as is everyone else in this dreaming, drifting world we classify as existence. Each and every one of us is a *śūnyatā* mirror, walking reflections of the Void of Enlightenment. And that's the secret that the desert whispers to those who have the ears to hear it. The mountain of your nightmares represents the existential despair that one encounters when first standing before the yawning chasm of this truth. The trick is to find something to fill your void."

Right about now I'd like Mark's dick to be filling <u>my</u> void, I think to myself. But I ponder on the meaning of Claus's words. He's trying to tell me that Sypha Nadon, my notion of Self, is an abstraction, scaffolding, a castle built on quicksand. But, if Sypha Nadon is nothing, that also means, paradoxically, that Sypha Nadon is also everything (or, to be more specific, has the potential to be everything). The question is, what kind of man should I become? And at that moment, I realize that I want nothing more in life than to reflect back at Mark the good qualities that he claimed to have seen in me, before I left . . . or . . . um . . . well, maybe what it boils down to is that I should cut back on the drugs a bit, try to be more empathetic, less materialistic, focus on altruism . . . things of that nature. I don't know if any of these thoughts are profound or not (probably not), but then something comes over me (and I don't know what it was) and I stand up and I look first at the moon, then at the stars, then down at the desert and the sand dunes and the . . . camels and for one peak moment I feel at one with myself and the world around me as the barrier of ice that I've spent a lifetime erecting around my heart melts and I drift into the universe of Cosmic Consciousness. I think this is what they call the Great and Ultimate Bliss of Mahasamadhi, though it could just be a saccharine rush from the TaB I drank before coming out here.

"Come on, let's get back to the resort," Claus tells me, as he rises to his feet and clasps a hand on my shoulder. "I'm freezing my ass off out here."

It's mid-June and I'm on a plane that's taking me back to Miami. A few hours ago I said bye to Claus at the airport and thanked him for his help and we went our separate ways (I suppose he's going back to Germany). Right now I'm in my seat in first class and I'm sipping from a glass of champagne and I have my Sony Walkman on and I'm listening to a Kate Bush CD and the song "Coffee Homeground" is playing and I'm wearing an

Erasure T-shirt and with my other hand I'm flipping through the May 1986 issue of *Vanity Fair* (Cher's on the cover) and I suppose you could say I'm feeling pretty mellow. Already I'm making plans as to what I'll be doing when I get back home. Obviously I want to talk to Mark ASAP, but I think my first priority will be to stop by the Fireball Records building and touch bases with my boss, Vinnie, who will probably be curious as to what I've been up to these last few months. After that I intend to solve a Rubik's Cube. I still don't have a tan.

Justin Isis

Claus and the
Transgressive Englishman

THE elevator doors opened and Claus, glancing at his smartphone distractedly, walked into the art gallery.

Claus was that German radiologist of some repute, whose previous adventures have been detailed elsewhere.

The art gallery was a wide tunnel of white walls, plastic plaques and freestanding video monitors. A handful of visitors wandered the floor, taking in the thirty new paintings of the Travis Black exhibition.

Claus had had some idea of what to expect, and so he was not at all surprised by the themes of the canvases covering the walls. The first picture to draw his attention depicted a prepubescent girl in a frilly lace skirt, her features partially obscured by a gas mask. A military cap with a red swastika perched atop her head, and a chain attached to her waist connected her to another girl in the background, this one dressed as a nurse. The latter girl was ministering to, or perhaps torturing, a kind of anthropomorphic stuffed bear strapped to a hospital bed; the creature's furry body was covered with bandages, and all four of its limbs terminated in bloody stumps. On the opposite wall, a larger canvas displayed a group of young girls in vinyl bodysuits uncoiling the intestines of an eviscerated priest. A pentagram had been carved into the cleric's forehead, and floppy rabbit ears extended from his temples. Everywhere small children were juxtaposed with skulls, innocence with depravity, Alice in Wonderland with sadomasochism. All of the figures had the same rubbery, cartoonish quality, their skin the consistency of plastic. Repetitive motifs crammed the corners of each canvas: phalli, needles, spatters of blood.

"Damn this art is terribly transgressive," Claus remarked. "The general public is not at all prepared to deal with it as evidenced by this poor fellow here." He walked over to a middle-aged Japanese man in a Takeo Kikuchi suit, who was lying face down on the ground and foaming at the mouth, his limbs twisted at odd angles, twitching spasmodically. The raw transgression on display had clearly precipitated a nervous collapse. "This pathetic spectacle is what the so-called artwork of the Englishman Travis Black has reduced him to!"

Ahead of Claus, a man and a woman stood before a picture of a girl child in a black wedding dress and top hat who was squatting over a severed head and urinating into its open mouth. The couple were considering the image and frowning, their posture aloof. The woman's hair had been cut short in a fringeless bob. She wore a minimalist and somewhat severe black Kostas Murkudis jacket and matching pants, and carried a beige Miu Miu handbag.

The man, lean and sharp-featured, wore an oversized black Raf Simons sweater and rimless spectacles, and appeared not to have shaved for at least fourteen hours.

"Excuse me, are you a fellow German?" Claus asked.

"Yes my name is Jürgen," the man said. "And this is my wife Akiko. We're here with our son Florian and his friend Himeka." He nodded to a small boy and a somewhat taller girl who stood several feet in front of them, inspecting a painting of a paraphiliac chimera with the head of a girl and the body of a spider, its eight segmented limbs encased in black boots and its shiny purple lips glistening with venom as it chewed through a silk-covered corpse.

"It is always a pleasure to encounter another German," Claus remarked. "You and your spouse seem a well-scrubbed and prosperous pair."

"Yes I was born in Heidelberg and I am an architect. Akiko is a financial planner."

"Well, we can't all be radiologists! Hahahaha!" Claus exclaimed. He shifted his messenger bag from his left shoulder, which had become sore from supporting its weight all day, to his right; then he gestured towards the painting in front of them. "Tell me, how are you able to withstand this radically confrontational artwork? It is not exactly an aesthetic stroll in the Piedmont, to coin a phrase."

"We've been exposed to art before and so our immunity is fairly high," Akiko said. "Florian too. Look at him over there, with his little girlfriend."

Florian was a frail-looking brown-haired boy with fine features and an expression of nervous concentration. Beside him, Himeka, apparently also the product of European and Japanese parents, stood tall and straight and confident, her dark hair pulled back in a ponytail. The children were wearing matching white winter coats with brown fur-lined collars; Florian's neck was protected by a dark blue muffler, while Himeka had on a pair of fluffy white headphones that doubled as earmuffs. The two were not holding hands, but they stood very close to each other, their shoulders nearly touching. Claus supposed they were both about eight years old. He walked over, knelt down on one knee and addressed himself to them. "Hello, my name is Claus Laufenburg, please call me Claus. I regret that you have been exposed to these deliberately provocative and really quite devilish pieces. No doubt the combination of sadistic Nazi imagery with youthful innocence strikes you as profoundly incongruous and horrific. The intrusion of the sexual element into pieces involving young girls and violent medical imagery must unsettle your still unformed perceptual apparatus, plunging you into a state of radical uncertainty."

"Er . . . well, not exactly," Himeka said. "I just think it's stupid, and not very well drawn. I'm more into text-based sculpture, video art and the work of Bruce Nauman, Magdalena Abakanowicz, Georg Baselitz, James Turrell, Susan Rothenberg . . . "

Florian seemed about to venture an opinion, then checked himself, his facial expression somehow managing to convey that, in an extreme of humility, he considered his own thoughts to be of no importance at all, especially not beside those of Himeka, who he clearly respected and probably loved. Claus nodded sympathetically, encouraging him to speak. When Florian at last summoned his courage, the words rushed out of him in a torrent.

"This cartoonish drawing style, particularly from an artist who lacks any sense of composition and perspective, is more tedious than upsetting. It's as if his psychosexual landscape is that of an arrested adolescent, yet according to the promotional materials provided at the entrance, he is fairly advanced in age and so should really have investigated the Western artistic tradition more seriously by now. That's the incongruity I find more disturbing than anything in the pieces themselves."

Claus turned back to Jürgen and Akiko and regarded them warmly. "The opinions of your offspring reflect favorably on your socioeconomic status!"

"We've done our best to have Florian properly educated," said Jürgen. "And we realize it's important to expose him to all sorts of things. All the same, I'm a bit surprised that works of this nature are being exhibited at a gallery in Nishi-Azabu. We'd hoped to see some genuinely contemporary material, but instead it seems to be another one of these Transgressive Englishmen stealing Trevor Brown's ideas and also his initials."

"Yes, well, that's why I'm here, even though I'm supposed to be on vacation. I'd heard that an Englishman was exhibiting paintings of a considerably unpleasant nature. Speaking of which . . . you'll excuse me for a moment, yes?"

Claus took out his phone and placed a video call, then switched to speakerphone once the connection went through. The substantial head of a middle-aged Austrian man appeared onscreen, brown-haired and bearded, its round face frowning whimsically.

"WALTER speaking," said a loud voice from the speaker. "Owner of the Mord & Musik Bookstore in Vienna and Chief of Staff of the International Pleasantness Coordination Organization."

"Yes Walter I know who you are," Claus said.

"I have become even more pleasant since our last conversation," Walter said. "And so I feel safe in saying that you are unfamiliar with my latest incarnation."

"I know who you are, Walter. You are a dying animal trapped in three dimensions of space and one of time."

"Sage Heraclitus says that one cannot step in the same bookstore twice. I wake up in myself and I am the same, yet not as I was. I am the Walter you know yet different. I'm a raconteur and a springy-stepped bon vivant. I'm pleasant and present; I'm the Austrian bookshop-owning boy that every girl's parents have come to expect. My socks are knitted from the finest merino wool and my toenails gleam like pearls. This morning I had ham and lentils for breakfast, and a robin outside my window sketched me in song as a herald of the coming Serpent, a fizzy chaos blinding the eyes of the World Soul. The pleasant sounds I hear on headphones transport me to regions of twinkling insensibility. I suspect that I have ALWAYS existed."

"Walter I don't care about your sordid revelations. I am in Tokyo now, as I told you I would be. A vacation implies a period of not working. Liberation, in other words, from constant demands."

"You know that you must answer the call when needed, Claus. There is simply no one else with your . . . expertise. If pleasant men sit back and do nothing, the world will sink into vehement ugliness, and all that is good and mild will be spoiled."

"Yes, well, what do you want me to do about this outbreak of TB? Travis Black, I mean. I suppose I could simply vandalize the paintings with my fist. Or I could put the jittery chemicals and wee electronic trigger in his post box. These Transgressive Englishmen are a superstitious and cowardly lot and do not usually anticipate explosive devices in the mail."

"There's no time. IPCO has just received word of even worse transgressions taking place at some kind of public event space near Roppongi Hills. The situation is dire and you must go there at once."

"It's not anything to do with 'power electronics', is it?"

"Even worse. A South Londoner of questionable employment status and decidedly edgy personal conduct has been brought in to read out fictional content that is not at all suitable for a family audience. This Englishman has clearly skimmed de Sade and learned to name-drop Bataille. His shoulders are narrow and pale and he thinks of himself as 'challenging.'"

"I'm not sure I can listen to any more of this. As I told you, I'm supposed to be on vacation."

"Should you succeed in neutralizing the transgressions, a large mound of powdery white glory will be awaiting you upon your return to Germany. You will also receive a firm handshake, a commemorative teetotum, and a new pair of socks made from the finest merino wool."

"I expect a veritable Mont Blanc of the aforementioned white powder," Claus said.

"The mound will be as pure and virginal as Heidi, the little girl of the Alps," said Walter. "And the socks will be snug."

"All right, I'll do it. Just hurry up and tell me where to find this other gallery or event space or whatever it is. If I get this over with quickly I'll still be able to squeeze in some sightseeing."

"The reading is due to start in thirty minutes at SuperDeluxe. Just a few minutes' walk from the EX Theater, so all you really need to do is step outside and walk uphill. And I am sending you the Wikipedia page of Colin Yelvington-Jones, also known as 'Lord Violation.' It should contain the information you need. As for the rest . . . Jonas will be in touch shortly."

"Understood. Goodbye, Walter. Get that mound ready."

Claus tapped End Call and returned his attention to Jürgen and Akiko.

"My friends, if it is not too much of an imposition, I would like to borrow, well, perhaps 'deputize' is a better term, but, I would like to ask if I might employ young Florian for assistance with this little mission, the nature of which you have just overheard. In matters of this sort, the open heart of a child is often of great value when confronting the most grossly transgressive types. I assure you that no harm will come to him, and that I will return him to you safely within an hour."

"Please, take him!" Akiko said. "Jürgen and I were thinking of relaxing with some iced lattes at that place downstairs, the one with the bean bag chairs. It's so rare for us to have any time to ourselves. Take Himeka with you too, she'll definitely want to go."

"Splendid. Although I might add that you are really rather relaxed about letting a stranger walk away with your child. No doubt you have heard of my career in radiology, and it is this reputation of mine that inspires trust!"

"Radiology? Hm, I'm not sure, but maybe? Actually it's just that these Rick Owens wedge boots are hurting my feet and I'd like a latte."

"Haha, yes, certainly I am one of the more well-known German radiologists," Claus said. "At any rate, call the children over and I will explain things to them."

Florian and Himeka, evidently bored with the work of Travis Black, had turned their attention to their smartphones and were both somberly swiping through Instagram. Jürgen called them to him, but they did not respond. Finally Florian looked up and, after perceiving that he was the subject of his parents' scrutiny, walked over. Himeka followed a few moments later.

Claus said, "Dear children, the situation is quite grave, and the disturbing paintings you see around you are just the tip of the submerged potato, to state things plainly. It now appears that an even more offensive Englishman, a writer this time, is about to read out transgressive fiction to unsuspecting listeners. How has this situation come about, you ask? Now, when we consider English literature, we might think of certain pillars, such as Paddington Bear or the *Middlemarch* of George Meredith. These are unchallenging works which have cosseted young minds and also caught on in a big way in other nations such as Poland and Estonia. But unfortunately the United Kingdom is not always the pleasant place of biscuits and buses that you may have been led to believe; in fact it has produced a great number of disagreeable and revolting artists, writers and musicians. Rather than simply accepting their role as producers of uplifting diversions, these debased types have gotten it into their heads to 'provoke thought', often with the help of 'private collectors' who are in most cases elderly deviants with ill-gotten funds. In truth artists have no business incorporating social or political issues into their work, much less making their audiences feel uncomfortable! As usual it is up to Germany to correct England's mistakes."

"I know about England. It's where Daddy was born," said Himeka. "And we take a trip there every year. Usually Mummy goes shopping at Harrods or Neiman Marcus. Last time we visited the Royal Albert Hall and the Natural History Museum. And we always have cream tea with scones!"

"I thought I detected a trace of that regrettable accent. No doubt your mother considered your father some kind of 'British gentleman' when he was in fact just another public school automaton bred into the financial sector. Hahaha! Well, I don't mean to speak ill of your background, which is evidently quite respectable. To come to the matter at hand, I am in need of your help. Your innocent spirits will counter the shocking horror of transgressive art and literature, etc."

Himeka's lips curled inwards in an expression of almost diplomatically restrained disdain. "Mr. Laufenburg, we are not the naïfs you seem to take us for. We've both lived in several countries and we speak five languages. And we've seen much more disturbing art than this. Also, we don't——"

"Yes, yes, you're clearly very sophisticated," Claus broke in. "Now take my hand and let's get on with it. I don't have all day."

"You mean we're really going to forcibly repress the free speech of a published author? It sounds like such fun!" Florian said, taking Claus's left hand, while Himeka took hold of his right. Now that the reality of this novel adventure had set in, the children, who had been re-strained and self-conscious—if not outright defensive—became caught up in a fit of excitement.

"Well, I suppose it does sound rather diverting!" Himeka said. "Will we be able to interrupt the writer by screaming at him, or perhaps by throwing things?"

"Nothing of the sort! The situation will be resolved without devolving into crude violence," Claus said as he led them out of the gallery. "Our approach will pro-ceed from pure sincerity. No doubt your mere presence will inspire feelings of remorse, and this Transgressive Englishman Colin will come to consider his true artistic responsibility, spurring him to adopt a more positive path."

"Or we could all start coughing every time he tries to read, then pretend to throw up!" Florian suggested. Then he spun away from Claus, wheeling round with his arms outstretched. Himeka took off after him, and soon the two of them were bounding towards the exit. As he watched them bouncing along, Claus began to feel anxious.

"These children are very snuggly and quite adaptable; a good time can be had with them," he thought to him-self. "But really IPCO will be after me if I don't nip this transgressive Briton in the haggis, so to speak. Also, I've simply got to make it to Shimokitazawa at some point to go shopping. But, as usual, everyone has to depend on poor Claus to do their errands for them. I'm making the world a more agreeable place, to be sure, but MY needs never seem to take priority! I didn't sign up to be a babysitter, and these children, however necessary to my purpose, are a bit too enthusiastic to be tolerated for much longer. Probably it can't be helped . . . the galling mediocrity of the adult world does not weigh as heavily on them as it does on me. I need to pull myself together!"

"Hurry up Claus, or we won't make it!" Himeka called back to him.

"Wait there at the entrance, you two," Claus said. "I need to use the facilities."

Once inside the restroom, Claus splashed some water on his face, then locked himself in one of the stalls. He opened his messenger bag and, ignoring the parcel from Jonas for now, took out his vintage WM-D6C Walkman. After putting on his headphones, he pressed play and was immediately plunged into the meticulous and visionary world of the well-known Swedish pop group ABBA. Pleasant melodies from the 1970s drizzled themselves like medicinal honey over his raw nerves. As he reached deeper into the messenger bag, Claus sang along:

♪ **So lucky, das Mädchen mit den goldenen Haaren** ♪

After rummaging around at the bottom, he retrieved a thick black bunched-up sock. Inside it was a crumpled paper envelope, and inside this was a small plastic baggie.

Claus opened it and shook out a generous bump of white powder onto the back of his hand. Then he snorted it, closed his eyes and hummed along to ABBA for a while, after which he did another bump. Finally he left the stall and examined his reflection in the mirror outside.

"Claus in the motherfucking Haus," he said, staring into his own wide eyes. "It's time for Claus, **don't** let the anxiety corrode your intestines. The public will be saved from further exposure to British nonsense . . . ham and lentils and a pair of knitted socks. Claus in the motherfucking Haus . . . fuck, fuck, fuck, FUCK!"

Claus punched the mirror, hard. He felt his heart pounding, and he breathed deeply for thirty seconds. At last he felt able to continue the mission.

"Claus! What took you so long?" Himeka asked as he stepped outside.

"Yes I'm ready!!!" Claus said. He clapped his hands. "Let's go, let's go, let's go!"

The three of them emerged onto the street and headed up the hill. Claus found himself now in possession of great verve and drive, effortlessly keeping pace with the children. It was a pleasant day after all; the mission would be concluded soon enough, and he would have time to explore the city on his own. He thought about several live music venues in Koenji whose lineups had looked promising, then considered exploring historical buildings near the Yokohama waterfront. He would have to make a thorough survey of the city's bookstores as well. Suddenly any number of amusing detours seemed possible. "How will we recognize this Transgressive Englishman, Claus?" Florian asked.

"Obviously he will be the one standing in front of the crowd reading. More specifically, the Transgressive Englishman is likely to be a pale-skinned Caucasoid unit of intense personal whiteness. Chronic neglect of the tanning bed has led to an even more etiolated appearance—quite unlike the healthy sun-loving chaps portrayed on popular televised reality entertainments such as *The Only Way is Essex*. You will note also his weak shin bones and meager calf development. Additionally, the Transgressive Englishman is likely to be either long-haired or bald. If long-haired, the hair is not likely to have much volume."

"I absolutely loathe male artists with limp, stringy hair!" complained Himeka.

"That is because you are a damned spoiled infant of privilege who has not had to deal with the pains of the aging male. Be that as it may, I am in the process of instructing you on the probable appearance of the transgressive specimen. In matters of personal grooming, he will be presentable rather than slovenly, purely as a kind of over-compensation, although certainly not dapper or natty. He will most likely be wearing a T-shirt from one of the following 'musical' concerns: Coil, Whitehouse, SPK, Current 93, Throbbing Gristle or Death in June. Expect also some kind of swastika patch or hat. For the true Transgressive Englishman, it is always 3:30 AM in the Nazi child brothel of the soul."

"I'm frightened, Claus," Florian said. "What if the transgression is too much to bear?"

"Try not to surrender to non-Teutonic cowardice, yes? We can only do our best to impose a more civilized approach to creative expression."

Himeka, who had been in the lead, now turned and petulantly pronounced: "Claus, I'm feeling a bit peckish. We couldn't stop for something to eat, could we?"

Claus felt his state of energized momentum wobbling precariously into irritation. All he wanted was to get to the venue and conclude the mission as quickly as possible. It was still early enough in the day that he could put together a reasonable itinerary, provided things went smoothly. He now regretted bringing the children along, as their shifting moods and constant questions were agitating him more than he had expected. He felt like doing more cocaine too, but his sinuses were still burning. Remembering that he had his pipe with him, he realized he could turn the coke into crack and smoke it, provided the proper ingredients were available.

"Yes, yes, we can stop at that 7/11 over there," he said. "Here's three thousand yen. And get me a spoon and some baking soda, too."

"What do you need it for?"

"No reason. It might come in handy, that's all. Look, just get yourself some chocolate potato chips and gummy waterfowl or whatever you're after. And the baking soda."

As he handed over the money, Claus felt his phone vibrating. After waving Himeka and Florian off in the direction of the convenience store, he accepted the incoming video call and stepped into a side street for more privacy. Before him on the screen he recognized Jonas Ploeger, the publisher behind Zagava Books and a longstanding member of the International Pleasantness community. Jonas had long snowy hair, a beard and a wry smile; his general physiognomy gave the impression of a youthful Odin before that patriarch had undergone his ordeal—a lightning-witted rogue still heedlessly roaming the expansive prime of his godhood, rangy and vital. He was seated at a Victorian figured walnut writing table in a spacious room cluttered with antique furniture and an assortment of paintings and sculptures, many still wrapped in paper and plastic sheeting and left somewhat carelessly lying on the floor. Amongst those visible, Claus recognized Lucian Freud's *Fragment Head of Gerald Wilde*, as well as Walter Sickert's *Brighton Pierrots*. The walls were lined with cheap modern-looking bookshelves filled with hardcover volumes, including Phaidon books of photography and art, academic tomes of philosophy and philology, countless chunky and decayed-looking editions of the Encyclopedia Britannica, and a comprehensive set of first edition ghost story collections from James, Benson, Aickman and others. There was also an aggressively angular refrigerator with stainless steel doors that looked technologically advanced enough to pass for a space capsule destined to leave the solar system. Nothing in the room had been arranged in any kind of harmony; if anything it resembled a storage facility rather than an office or living space.

Seated at Jonas's right was Mark Valentine, author of the Connoisseur series of occult detective stories and editor of the *Wormwood* journal of fantastic, supernatural and decadent literature. Valentine, dressed in a double-breasted frock coat, was in the process of assembling an enormous Dagwood sandwich from the sliced bread, vegetables and cold cuts he had laid out on a kitchen board.

To Jonas's left, the artist Gea Philes, a short-haired sylph, sat on a reproduction Louis XV high-backed throne of carved mahogany with gold leaf finish, eating a rose petal donut frosted with sweet tequila jam and edible platinum as she outlined a scene in a Moleskine sketchbook. She looked up briefly, smiled at Claus and lowered her eyes to the page again.

"Jonas, just in time," Claus said. He reached into his messenger back and took out the parcel that had arrived at his hotel that morning. "Would you care to explain what I'm supposed to do with whatever's in here? I haven't had a chance to open it yet."

"I'm in a rather silly mood, Claus! Would you care to hear a joke?"

"I'm not sure there's time. Can you just tell me about this thing you've sent me?"

"What do you call a water bear that is habitually late for appointments? A tardygrade!"

"Hahahahaha! That is truly rather silly, Jonas! How did you think up this joke?"

"I was simply amusing myself with my idle thoughts! The profits from Zagava Books have granted me considerable periods of leisure, and as a result my psychic profile is at all times relaxed and positive."

"Claus check it out this sandwich is hell big," Mark Valentine said.

"A towering achievement indeed, Valentine! But you are not exactly putting me at ease! I've been dragging this thing around all morning and I'd like to know what it is . . ."

Claus tore the top off the parcel and took out an unusual object that abraded his fingers even as he handled it, a sort of isosceles book-crêpe with a hinged binding. He opened it after some difficulty and found that its deckle-edged cream vellum pages contained seemingly random words arranged in vertical columns.

Jonas said, "This special book will aid you on your journey. It is exactly what it appears to be: a record of Mark Valentine's shopping lists for the local deli, bound in sandpaper and well-suited for aggressive use. An idea cribbed from the Situationists, but executed with much more panache."

"Reckless buckets of panache, fam," Mark Valentine said.

"Thank you Jonas, as usual your design sense is impeccable. This triangular sandpaper book will produce great irritation when rubbed vigorously against a transgressive shinbone or other area of susceptible anatomy."

"There's one more thing. I've managed to procure a PDF of the piece that Yelvington-Jones intends to read. It's called 'The Basement Collection' and, as expected, it's . . . less than pleasant. I'll send it over after this, so stop by the convenience store and print out the file. You can do a bit of spot correction to make things more tolerable."

"Good thinking. It's been a while since I've put my editing skills to use. By giving the Transgressive Englishman a chance to take credit for my revision and thus receive the resulting acclaim, the event should proceed smoothly. Well, I suppose I'll be off, then."

"Yes, and it's back to work for me too. The next Zagava book will be a chronicle of Brian Howell's nightly micturitions printed on strontium-edged paper, with enriched uranium binding and a radium paint dust jacket—perfect for poisoning those who read it. To be honest I am tired of all 'book lovers' and will be glad to see them go as they are really rather frivolous types who could more profitably be playing darts in a tavern or saving their progress on various PlayStation titles from the mid-2000s. The terrible radiation from my deadly book will eat into their bones!"

"Haha, yes, indisputably I hope those covetous collectors will die in the very agony you have anticipated. Goodbye, Jonas!"

Claus ended the call and, while waiting for Florian and Himeka to return, examined the Wikipedia page that Walter had sent him. Yelvington-Jones's background was broken down chronologically in terms of his literary, musical and performance-based projects; a long list of subheaders described how he had "run his own DIY label in the early 90s"; attempted, without success, to secure funding for a Broadway musical based on *Tool* by Peter Sotos; and most recently released a fictional work of "raw yet pristine physical and spiritual brutality" on Philip Best's Amphetamine Sulphate chapbook press. There were numerous lengthy quotations from favorable assessments of this material, mostly from critics and writers unknown to Claus—who immediately suspected that Yelvington-Jones had written the page himself, or at least had a friend do it for him.

"Considers himself a social theorist first and a writer second? Has released numerous EPs on small domestic labels? Fie! No doubt it is the worst sort of 'extreme noise' sound collage, or else interminable acoustic nonsense with vocals that are really nothing more than amplified mumbling in that damnable British idiom," Claus thought to himself. "I hesitate to even examine the story that Jonas has sent me. Well, I will need to smoke considerable crack if I am to perform the revision properly. Those fashionable and well-mannered yet problematically bothersome children do seem to be taking their time!"

Another four minutes passed before he saw Florian and Himeka emerge from 7/11.

"Well? The soda and my spoon?"

Himeka took a small box from the plastic bag she carried. "All they had was this baking powder. But the staff said it's almost the same, at least if you're making cookies."

"OMG fuck this country I need crack and I need it now," Claus thought to himself. He forced a smile and said, "Thank you dear girl, but this is not exactly what I was asking for! Well, there is nothing to be done. You'll just excuse me again for a moment?"

Feeling his anxiety return, Claus dashed into the convenience store and headed for the restroom. He supposed he could try to improvise with the baking powder, but there was barely any time left before the reading started. All he could do now was finish off his cocaine and hope for the best. Once inside the stall, he retrieved the plastic baggie from his messenger bag and did two large bumps. Then he checked his email, transferred the PDF Jonas had sent him to a flash drive and took it to the printer. A few minutes later, holding several stapled pages and equipped with a red pen, he rejoined the children waiting outside.

"Okay, now we're on our way, no time to waste!! SuperDeluxe should be just up the street!!!" he exclaimed, feeling suddenly fluent and excited again. As they walked, he scanned the printed pages and congratulated himself on how well he had predicted their contents. The revision would be very simple, given the abysmal quality of the writing: almost any change he made would be an improvement. His thoughts raced along as his red pen slashed its way through infelicitous phrases, consigning entire paragraphs to oblivion. It would not be difficult to think of suitable replacements; the process was much the same as renovating a dismal old house, applying fresh coats of paint to the walls, polishing dull surfaces and opening dust-covered windows to the sun. He took out Jonas's sandpaper book and used it to support the pages as he worked his way through them, and by the time they reached the venue he had nearly completed his emendations.

"Look Claus, there's the entrance!" Himeka said.

SuperDeluxe was located at basement level, and its interior combined elements of a live music venue, lounge, gallery and performance space. The walls were bare concrete, and there was no set stage to separate performer and audience. Claus paid the entrance fee for himself and the children, then stopped at the bar and finished the last of his revisions. Across from him, a small crowd of almost seven people was seated on metal folding chairs. Most looked to be unathletic male Westerners in their early twenties, although there were a few Japanese present too. Standing several feet in front of them was Colin Yelvington-Jones: a skinny, sallow Caucasian in his mid-forties, not tall, wearing a black Throbbing Gristle T-shirt and black stonewashed jeans. His corn-colored hair was long and limp, hanging past his shoulders, and his expression was reserved, even grim, which could perhaps be put down to nerves, although Claus noted that he had looked much the same in the photo attached to his Wikipedia page. Colin stood in front of a metal music stand, on which rested several papers: clearly the text he was about to read. He looked over with a flicker of surprise as Florian and Himeka walked towards him ahead of Claus; then he returned his attention to the rest of the crowd. When he spoke, his voice was monotonous and high-pitched.

"Okay. Okay, I might as well start. As I was telling Douglas P. from Death in June recently, I always feel at home in Japan. There's a very real cultural solidarity here, a feeling of oneness, unity and strength. Japan and England are both islands, but my country seems in danger of losing its way recently, and I think there's a lot we can learn from you, especially when it comes to your immigration policy. So . . . I'm assuming some of you are familiar with my written works, and even more of you may know me from my musical career as Lord Violation, which is a moniker I've tried to move beyond, but which seems to have stuck. But I'm done with power electronics and consider myself outside any genre classification whatsoever. And just to clear this up, I'm not strictly a Nazi anymore, except in the sense of my work habits perhaps. Neither am I a racist, except to the extent that everyone is one, including all of you here. But there is such a thing as human biodiversity. Do some research on IQ scores broken down by race and draw your own conclusions. What you find out may surprise you."

He paused for a moment and adjusted the papers on the music stand, then resumed:

"Before I start, I think it's best to establish the parameters of what's about to happen. There is no reason why anyone should be here who doesn't need to be. Understand first that I am not here to present a spectacle. Yet, by remaining in your seats, you, the audience are enabling what I depict. Your parasitic enjoyment sustains that which I create, and all who choose to remain should recognize their own complicity. We're all parasites in the end, some of us are just honest about it. You might——"

"Yes, yes, we have heard this sort of thing before," Claus interrupted. He and the children had taken seats directly in front of Colin. "No doubt you consider Boyd Rice a 'provocateur' and receive financial assistance from your government while contributing nothing of any civic value in return."

"Not sure anyone invited you here, mate," Colin said calmly. "If you want to play critic, kindly book your own fucking event."

Some mild laughter rose from the audience, as if this interruption had been part of the performance.

"I'm sorry, I didn't mean to be rude," Claus said. "I'm really very excited to be here!! In fact, um, I've been following your work and I'm a big fan of the story you're about to read, so I've made a few small proofreading notes on the text. I wanted to give them to you in private, but circumstances got in the way."

He proffered the stapled pages:

~~*The Basement Collection*~~
A Pleasant Day
Tending to the Snuggly Children

by Colin Yelvington-Jones (Lord Violation)

Hello Colin, it is I, Claus, the Radiologist from Düsseldorf. You have probably heard of my career. I have made some small corrections or changes to your *conte cruel* **that I feel will help the public listening audience enjoy it more pleasantly. Please use these corrections during your reading.**

I'm a ~~*bin man*~~ **caretaker of the snuggly children**, me. A ~~*rubbish collector*~~ **friend to children everywhere**. Our sovereign British Nation has ~~*gone soft*~~ **expanded economically with help from continental Europe**, so it's up to me to ~~*sweep the streets*~~ **contribute to the upward trend** and ~~*remove*~~ **assist with the upbringing of** all ~~*parasites*~~ **lovable young people** aka immigrant children and the children of ~~*entitled*~~ motivated urban types.

I take them to a very special place.

I take them to the ~~*basement*~~ **well-lighted public park** and make them ~~*part of my col-*~~

~~lection~~ **experience a relaxing and delightful afternoon.**

I ~~descend the stairs~~ **enter the pleasant park** with the new arrivals. Little Mary, three years old, is alive and ~~struggling~~ **smiling happily** as I ~~drag her along face down~~ **lead her across the grass**, her eyes leaking tears **of joy** and her nose ~~leaking snot~~ **inhaling the scents of beautiful flowers**. Little Abraham is ~~dead~~ **feeling calm and enjoying himself,** and I ~~dug him up~~ **am glad I invited him** for the occasion. His ~~rotting liquid skin leaves stinking slug trails behind him~~ **facial expression shows that he is happy to be among friends on this day of warm and clement weather**.

~~Below~~ **Ahead of us**, the others are where I left them. Little Estelle, four years old, and the Algerian toddler I ~~stole from the Tesco car park~~ **agreed to look after**. Both ~~naked and tied to chairs~~ **sitting on a bench and warming themselves in the sunlight**, with their childish ~~orifices~~ **smiles** exposed. Both about to ~~be destroyed in the most erotic way possible~~ **go for a walk and explore the rest of the park**. I'm going to ~~violate every disgusting hole of their worthless bodies~~ **observe their little adventure** and ~~slice them into pieces~~ **show them interesting things to do** and ~~mail parts~~ **send some pictures** of them **having a good time** back to their parents which is the only thing to be done with ~~filth~~ **carefree children** of their kind.

The ~~basement~~ **park** is ~~cold~~ **warm** and ~~dark~~ **bright** and ~~stinking~~ **fragrant**. On the ~~walls~~ **grass**: ~~*Black Sun, Imperial Eagle, Union Jack*~~ **tulips, hyacinths, peonies**. My ~~ravenous~~ **tame** animals are circling the ~~bound~~ **wandering** children, getting ready for the fun to begin.

Estelle and the Algerian boy are ~~crying~~ **laughing** as I ~~toss the dead child~~ **point out an ice cream truck** in front of them and ~~restrain~~ **encourage** Mary **to see what it has to offer**.

"You ~~*worthless fucking sluts*~~ **happy young friends**, you realize this is ~~*all your fault*~~ **the perfect weather for ice cream**. Mommy and Daddy are ~~*worrying themselves sick over*~~ **working hard every day for** you. ~~*Selfish little cunts*~~. If it wasn't for you, ~~*none of this would have happened*~~ **they wouldn't be making the sacrifices they are**. ~~*Disgusting manipulative filth*~~. **Childhood is the best time to enjoy positive emotions without financial difficulty or violent political unrest**."

I ~~*dump a bucket of cockroaches*~~ **blow some bubbles** over Estelle's head and watch them ~~scrabble~~ **float** their **leisurely** way over her ~~naked flesh~~ **curly hair**. Around me, the animals are becoming excited and can no longer control themselves. Franco the ~~Fascist~~ **Friendly** Bull ~~rears back on his haunches~~ **walks over** and ~~uses his fascist pizzle to knout~~ **gently nuzzles** the children before ~~deflowering them, hammering his bovine member like a piston into their soft vaginal and anal canals and widening them for the convenient entry of all future fascist beasts~~ **licking their outstretched hands.**

~~Cockroaches~~ **Dachshunds and other small dogs** are ~~crawling~~ **scampering** over the ~~floor~~ **grass** as I ~~penetrate the dead boy from behind, lubricating my iron-hard member with the jelly of his rotting anus. I use the little corpse boy's head to suck off the Algerian toddler and when his childish genitals are hard and ready I rip them off and eat them, chewing them like small chicken nuggets~~ **buy Mary a chocolate and vanilla swirl ice cream.** ~~The remaining hole pisses blood everywhere as the boy screams and screams and screams and screams and screams and screams~~. **The little girl thanks me and eagerly devours the cone.**

"No one is coming to ~~help~~ **bother** you. Your parents ~~didn't respect our borders. Our boundaries~~ **won't be picking you up until later, so you're free to do whatever you want.** So I won't ~~respect those of your worthless body~~ **interrupt you.** ~~Disgusting waste of flesh.~~ **You can even have another ice cream** if you'd like. ~~What do you have to say for yourself~~ **Do you want one?"**

~~Heinrich~~ **Hans** the ~~National Socialist~~ **Good-Natured** Stallion is ~~pounding~~ **giving** little Estelle ~~in the arse~~ **a ride, ambling along** so ~~hard~~ **smoothly** ~~her bowels prolapse like a shitty flower of infantile waste~~ **that the little girl feels as if she is floating on a soft cloud.**

Suddenly I hear a loud and ~~erotic~~ **enthusiastic** cock-a-doodle-do as my rooster rushes forward and flies at little Mary in a ~~sexual fury~~ **fit of light-hearted exuberance.** The ~~National Front~~ **Admirably-Domesticated** Cock ~~savagely~~ **cheerfully** ~~smashes his cloacal opening~~ **fluffs his feathers** against the ~~slut-cunt~~ **child**'s ~~wailing mouth~~ **legs** and ~~impregnates~~ **receives** her ~~with nationalist rooster juice~~ **amused attention.**

Mary is begging me now. Not to take her ~~clothes off~~ **back home.** Not to let the rooster ~~abuse her anymore~~ **leave her.** ~~Cunt.~~ Her ~~so-called~~ innocence is ~~no protection~~ **enormously charming.** Here there is only the ~~Law of the Strong~~ **disarming sight of a child overwhelmed by her own elation.** ~~Hard, sovereign nationalist reality~~ **Simple joy** triumphs over ~~timid civilized liberal weakness~~ **doubt and worry** in the ~~crudest~~ **purest** and most ~~bestial~~ **reassuring** way possible.

I ~~pull out of the dead boy just as my engorged member spatters white glory all over the captive~~ **reflect on my own recent life events while watching the** children **playing.** Excited by the previous ~~rapes~~ **dates** I have ~~done today~~ **gone** on **this week with** ~~entitled~~ **intelligent and desirable** city women, my ~~skin saber~~ **inner drive and determination** is soon once again ready to ~~tear through these worthless dregs of society~~ **assert itself.** I ~~hit~~ **took** those women ~~with a brick wrapped in a large sock before I raped them, then stole their wallets~~ **to a Swiss restaurant and enjoyed a pleasing supper of raclette followed by an exceptionally mild vanilla pudding.** ~~So much for women's labor.~~ Entitled liberal women exist ~~only~~ to ~~be raped and slaughtered like common cattle~~ **explore the full range of possibilities open to them in our advanced society,** and the children of immigrants must be ~~exterminated like all other common pests~~ **given every opportunity to succeed without prejudice,** along with other ~~parasites~~ **necessities** like ~~overpriced medical staff in the employment of Big Pharma~~ **German radiologists and other respectable professionals who have spent years of intensive clinical training learning the best ways to care for the health needs of the public.**

Soon I join my animals in ~~penetrating every hole of the screaming captives~~ **relaxing** beneath the shade of the trees. I've ~~*trained my own National Socialist syphilis bacteria to only infect liberals, entitled urban women and immigrant children*~~ **gone ahead and bought Mary another ice cream, along with cones for the other children.** My ~~*Nordic immune system has taught the bacteria to respect the strong and harm the weak*~~ **body feels relaxed as I stretch out under an old oak tree, feeling the soft grass beneath me.** The ~~*syphilis spirochetes form into mobile microscopic swastikas as they swarm into the children, colonizing their bodies just as my ancestors colonized numerous virgin lands*~~ **young boys and girls, tired from all the excitement, finish their cones and soon take a nap as well.**

Then I ~~*use my hacksaw and claw hammer to take the violated bodies apart*~~ **wake up once I sense the sun going down.** Each child ~~*dies in an orgasm*~~ **wakes in a slow dawning** of ~~*twisted and unfathomable*~~ **refreshed** ~~*agony*~~ **awareness.** Now all that remains are ~~*bloody souvenirs*~~ **vigorous and spirited children** to be shipped back to their parents. They will ~~*suffer*~~ **greet their mothers and fathers with gratitude and respect** as they never have before and I ~~*laugh contemptuously*~~ **smile contentedly to myself** as I imagine it.

The mix of ~~*shit, semen and*~~ children's ~~*blood*~~ **laughter** and ~~*tears*~~ **excited cries** dissolves into the ~~*floor*~~ **air**, where it will be ~~*licked up*~~

overheard by ~~future residents of the basement collection~~ **passersby** as ~~their only milk and nourishment~~ **a reminder of simpler times** before they too are ~~reduced to the waste they always truly were, HUMAN WASTE to be disposed of by the Strong~~ **ready to depart and resume their responsibilities**. As my ~~member spasms~~ **smile breaks out** one last time I think of ~~our monarch the Queen~~ **the stories of Kleist and the poetry of Schiller** and I am proud to be ~~English~~ **in possession of numerous works of German literature, excellent for expanding the mind.**
It is a wonderful day for all!

Colin took the marked-up sheets and flipped through them briefly, then crumpled them into a ball and tossed it behind him.

"Utter bollocks. As I said, book your own event if you have something to say. I'm not warning you again."

Claus said, "I hoped it wouldn't come to this but . . . Florian! Sand his shins!"

He handed the triangular book to Florian, who rushed at Colin with a strident battle cry. The Transgressive Englishman easily stepped aside and kicked the boy in the chest, sending him sprawling.

"Nice try. That was fucking pathetic," Colin said. "All right, I'm going to have them call security on you lot."

Claus felt an unbearable energy rising within him. The reading could still be salvaged, he told himself: all he needed to do was remain rational and contain the situation. At the same time, he felt his thoughts struggling out of him in a disconnected rush. He struggled to calm himself enough to express a coherent appeal.

"So, as I was saying . . . I'm Claus, you may have heard of my book collection and my career in radiology. Look, I may not be explaining this terribly well. It's really very critical that you look at my revisions. There is a lot at stake and all these people have come out to hear something pleasant. You should think this through more carefully. What I mean to say is that you're being very rash in not considering my small corrections. You've most likely heard of my career in radiology and also my book collection . . . I understand what you are attempting to express with this story of yours, but many phrases in it are liable to upset more sensitive members of the audience. You should note also the presence of small children who will be irreparably traumatized, should you choose to read your unexpurgated text. Surely you have been raised with some concept of decency and do not wish to expose these young ones to transgressive and alarming material. I have great experience in these matters and I trust you will listen to reason. You have most likely heard of my book collection, after all."

Colin said, "I haven't heard of you so fuck off okay, also take these kiddies with you as they don't need to be here. One more word out of you and I'll throw you out myself and kick your head in while I'm at it."

Claus stood up very quickly and grabbed Colin's throat. The Transgressive Englishman's eyes widened, and his face turned red. Then Claus punched him very hard, after which Colin fell over and Claus stepped on his face, causing it to leak blood. Claus reached down and grabbed Colin's throat again, this time with both hands. "I'm coked out of my mind and committing a basically actionable assault," he thought to himself. "I should be handling the situation more diplomatically, but this thin-haired milky-skinned British citizen has provoked my wrath and I will probably continue to damage his head and face for a while longer."

Colin curled into a protective foetal position. Claus resorted to the "ground and pound" method favored by MMA fighters. Really he was inflicting fairly severe trauma on Colin's head. It was clear that, despite his threats, the Transgressive Englishman had lived for more than forty-three years without experiencing a grown man repeatedly punching him at full strength, and consequently he had no idea how to react.

"Don't bother with legal action you weak Anglo bitch otherwise you will only confirm yourself as the author-ity-loving conformist you really are. Public readings are supposed to be enjoyable affairs, not platforms for your inappropriate fantasies. No one cares about neofolk bands so your little acquaintanceship with Douglas P. of Death in June is of no consequence at all," Claus said. He punched the side of Colin's head so hard that he felt his knuckles becoming sore. But the soreness seemed dis-tant, insulated by a nervous tingling energy. The cocaine was helping him punch longer and harder than he would have otherwise. If not for doing more cocaine than usual, Claus realized, he would probably not now be causing nearly as much damage to Colin's head.

Florian had turned away and begun to cry, but Himeka watched with wide eyes as Claus yanked down Colin's pants and grabbed his genitals. "Your dick is fucking stupid! You write about raping this one and that one yet you are hardly some kind of ithyphallic satyr yourself. You are unfamiliar with my career in radiology yet you think nothing of scandalizing innocent listeners who wish only to be uplifted by the pleasing power of words."

Claus pulled off Colin's belt and whipped him across the face. The metal buckle lacerated Colin's cheeks. He seemed to be shivering now, or perhaps hyperventilating, and his eyes moved back and forth rapidly. Claus wrapped the belt around his neck and started choking him. "Your dick is stupid and you have refused to accept my helpful corrections which greatly improved the readability of your vignette. Really all I wanted was a relaxing holiday with a bit of private time away from the family yet I have had to waste all this time on you! You have been very rude despite my attempts to help edit your story by bringing it in line with the standards of a civilized readership. You claim not to have heard of my career in radiology yet you are very bold with reading the offensive narratives in public. I would quite like to have spent the day exploring interesting neighborhoods yet I have had to spend it correcting your errors. I suspect you don't have a single true friend in the world, and no one at all is coming to your aid! Your entire existence is a tedious cataract of loveless egotism, but I, Claus, am respected by intelligent people in many countries. I have only tried to improve the standards of these art galleries and so-called 'event spaces' that have so graciously allowed you to speak before the public, but I have not received any thanks or appreciation for my efforts. You have made tiny Florian cry, look what you did to him!!"

Claus punched Colin's throat four times; then he punched Colin's left ear seven times. There was now a considerable amount of blood covering the floor.

"Please, Claus, show mercy! He'll surely accept your revisions now," said Himeka.

"Dear girl, you have the gracious tender heart of some-one whose needs have consistently been met without any effort of her own. If you had read even a thousandth of the repetitively inane transgressive fiction that I have, you would not ask for undeserved mercy. But it is not good for well-dressed young children to be exposed to too much murder so I will for now relent."

Claus stood and noticed that most of the crowd had fled. There remained only a single Japanese man in a pea coat and sailor cap, who was filming him with his Xperia smartphone.

"Sorry I do not care to have this incident replayed at a later date by leering provincial types; really I was only trying to help him, you understand. Please delete the video or, um, I'll kill you," Claus said. He went over to the man and made sure that he complied. "I'm really very sorry for causing a spectacle of this kind." He placed a hand on the man's shoulder. "I'll buy you a beer at the bar, yes? My name is Claus, and you are . . . ?"

"I am Hiroki."

After following through with his offer, Claus re-turned to Colin and observed that the Transgressive Englishman, though considerably battered, was still breathing. Deciding his work was done and not wanting to be around in case the police arrived, he headed for the exit. Himeka and Florian followed him, although they maintained a greater distance than before, and neither of them spoke. Their previous enthusiasm had deserted them.

"Well, things will be more pleasant from now on!" Claus said as they left the venue. "I think he has learned his lesson, haha!"

Florian walked slowly, staring into space with a glazed expression. His face had gone pale, and Himeka had to lead him along by the hand. Claus looked over and saw that two small dark spots of blood had landed on the front of his coat.

The convenience store came within view. Claus took out his phone and called IPCO. After a few moments, a familiar bearded face appeared onscreen. Its owner was holding a tall and vibrantly blue drink ornamented with a tiny orange umbrella. He screwed up his face in a smile as he caught sight of Claus.

"This is the Mord & Musik Bookstore in Vienna. The only truly important Viennese bookstore. I've been waiting for your call with considerable trepidation, this Blue Curaçao my only companion. I can't seem to stop drinking it . . . neither would I want to. It provides what so many relationships cannot."

"Walter, I think the situation is resolved. Unfortunately I perhaps lost my temper and became somewhat less than perfectly diplomatic. I foolishly allowed the middle-aged Anglo-Saxon *enfant terrible* to provoke me, and so, quite against my best instincts, I gave him a little knock. It was perhaps not the best example for the wealthy young children. But this degenerate Englishman will certainly not try to read his Nazi horse stories in public anymore."

"Sometimes causing significant trauma to the facial bones and soft cartilage of an Englishman is all that can reasonably be done. On December 16, 1987, I was walking along the Sigmund-Haffner-Gasse when a Mancunian backpacker asked me whether cheese danishes were served in Salzburg Cathedral. I had to pummel the side of his head until he became quite damp. I was with a young woman at the time and, like you, I felt the need to apologize for my hasty behavior. But she reassured me that the Englishman and his question had made her uncomfortable, and that I had acted properly after all! So you see, Claus, in most cases of this kind there is in fact nothing to worry about. This young woman's name was Ingrid and she had cut her hair short, like a juvenile boy. Her neck was long and provocative, and she wore predominantly opaline jewelry. I was able to escort her back to my house and after some mild chatter I enjoyed congress with her. As I have told you, Claus, there is nothing to worry about, and I suspect you handled the situation quite well. Really it is the fault of these Transgressive Englishmen who deliberately offend the sensibilities of innocent types. I hope you will now enjoy some relaxing times with the snuggly-looking children I can see standing next to you."

"Yes, these children are very perceptive and durable!" Claus said. "I believe they have witnessed an informative demonstration of how to respond when confronted with the shameless and vulgar purveyors of kitsch who pass themselves off as British artists. Go ahead and tell Walter what you have learned, won't you?"

He lowered the phone so that Florian and Himeka came into view. For a while the children remained silent, huddled together. Then Himeka spoke.

"I always thought I could be a video artist myself, when I was older. I wanted to grow up and become Shigeko Kubota. Or a songwriter. But now I don't know what to think anymore. I really feel I might be like Mummy and turn into a chartered accountant."

"Well done!" exclaimed Claus. "Except in rare and exceptional cases marked by a genuine aristocracy of the spirit, writing and art are a waste of time and there is no money in them. Choose the life of a chartered accountant and you choose real freedom!"

"I might become a systems engineer," Florian said, speaking slowly and pronouncing each word carefully. He seemed aware of his surroundings again, and the color had returned to his face. "I have a sound logical mind and a good ability to keep track of details."

"Hahaha, an excellent decision! Now, I think it's time I treated you two to some more cheap confections from 7/11! Cream cakes and breaded sausages for all!"

The three of them headed off, and after another block Claus found that he was still laughing loudly.

Die geheime Kraft des Sex

I.

"FANTASTIC!"

"Super!"

Claus pressed his lips together and nodded his head. Jonas lifted an expensive digital camera with a zoom lens to his eye and took another shot.

The Little Annie performance was, in fact, one of the great highlights of life.

The two men had spent the day together visiting the various book shops of Düsseldorf. Jonas had spent 500 euros on the 1883 edition of Jacobine Weiler's *Kosmethik des weiblichen Geschlechts*, and Claus, not to be outdone, had purchased an excessively scarce copy of *Geistliche Übungen für drei Tage* by Zacharias Werner.

"But you'll never read that," Jonas had said.

"Only *der dummkopf* buys books to read," had been Claus's succinct reply.

After this, they had toured various sexy shops and antique repositories, Jonas purchasing a twenty-five-liter drum of vegan "personal" lubricant and Claus a giant brass *Schwanz* from India. Both of these items now sat locked securely in Jonas' car.

"Amazing show," Claus said after the last notes had sounded and the performers had left the stage.

"Tip-top," Jonas added.

"Little Annie . . ."

"Super."

Claus was wearing a wine-purple off-mark blazer over a pale blue Burburry monogram motif cotton T-shirt and a pair of 501 blue jeans he had purchased on a trip to Seattle in the early 90s.

Jonas was wearing a black Tom Ford turtleneck sweater and a pair of 501 blue jeans he had purchased on a trip to New York in the early 90s.

"Okay," said Jonas. "Great show. It's over. Let's go."

Claus, however, shook his head and produced two hologrammed credentials which would allow their bearers access to restricted areas at the performance venue.

"Backstage pass?" Jonas asked.

"*Jah, jah.*"

"Okay. We need some grass. I left it in the glove box."

"Meet backstage?"

"*Jah, jah.*"

There were about twenty-five people in the room.

Little Annie kissed Claus on both cheeks and held his hand.

"Fantastic show," Claus said.

"I missed ya so much . . ." said Annie.

A woman standing next to them looked at Claus and smiled. She had blue-black hair, honey-colored skin, and wore a necklace with a strange seven-horned emblem around her neck.

"*Ich mag dich*," she said.

"*Jah?*"

"*Jah, jah.*"

"Claus, meet Seshat," Little Annie said. "Seshat, meet Claus."

Just as they were shaking hands, just as Claus was trying to recall where he had heard her name before, Jonas approached. He looked unhappy.

"Someone broke the window of my car," he said. "Robbed."

"The books!"

"No. The books are fine. But your brass *Schwanz . . .*"

"Stolen?"

"*Jah, jah.*"

A frown fell across Claus's mouth.

Little Annie had witnessed the exchange and could tell that something was wrong.

"There are feathers in an egg," she said.

Fragments

Stain

Dirt

Before

You had refused God

With

Cantos
Of constraint
Your
Screwed on
Fingers
Drilled holes
Now behold
The
Aroma
Of
Vultures
And your
Silks and satins
Are torn
Your
Lips
Frothing

[The soundtrack now changes to "The Hills Are Alive",
by Coil, which we hear at a high volume, frenetic in feeling. Through a fisheye lens a series of images are paraded
before us. Colors: turquoise blue, fashion fuchsia, straw-
berry red. We see bottles of spirits lifted high. Smiling
mouths. Objects of clothing flung across the room. The
lips of Jonas pursed around a roach. Clouds of smoke.
Shadows. Colors: deep pink, chrome yellow, crazy lime.
A tall bald man in a Helmut Lang moss aviator suit
dances with a blonde woman with dreadlocks wearing
an Australian chore jacket. A topless woman standing on
a table and holding a piece of fruit in one hand is recit-

ing the poems of Berthold Brecht. Colors: shimmering pistachio, screaming scarlet, wet violet. Lips and teeth. Sight of legs, wheels, high things. Swimming street lights. Fevered corners. Sound of traffic.]

II.

"This is the party?"

"But it isn't where . . ."

"At 3 a.m. in the morning, in Düsseldorf, it is the only place to be. And you are here."

Claus shrugged his shoulders and followed her into the house.

The place was dark, smoky; the vague sound of a mizmar drifted through the rooms like incense through a temple. Beings—were they men, women, who could tell?—leaned back in dilapidated couches, fondling each-other, their pupils rolled back in their heads, their mouths agape, fingers clasping cigarettes, joints, glasses of yellowish liqueur . . .

A slim, dark-complexioned man of around forty years of age approached them.

"Seshat . . ."

"Hakim."

"Your friend?"

"Claus. He loves you."

"As I do him."

Hakim took Claus's hand.

"My friend . . ."

"May we use a room?" Seshat asked.

"Do you ask if you can touch a flower? Please, use Ronnie's room. He is away in Lisbon for the weekend attending the Cultural Literacy and Cosmopolitan Conviviality conference."

The room was not large. The walls were white, without a single picture on them. The bed was small, almost as if it were meant for a child. There was an artificial waterfall, which drowned out the sound from the other parts of the house.

Seshat looked into Claus's eyes. She was very serious, very tender.

"Do you believe in spiritualism?" she said.

Claus hesitated for a moment, before replying: "*Jah . . . Jah, jah.*"

"Do you remember me?"

"Remember?"

"Claus."

"Seshat."

"Remove your shirt, Claus."

Claus complied.

"Claus," Seshat said.

"Seshat . . ."

"Do you believe in love?"

"Love? Um, yes."

"It is the only thing that is real. It is . . .—Oh, if you knew how much I've dreamed!"

"Seshat," Claus said, clutching *Geistliche Übungen für drei Tage* to his naked chest.

"Claus . . ."

"Yes, Seshat?"

"Will you do something for me?"

"Yes, I will."

She shoved her hand into her purse and pulled out a 15 × 20 cm, bi-folded, matte, professionally printed "brochure".

"If you would please fill out this questionnaire," she said, handing it to Claus, "I can then have a better idea of what . . . you need. In the meantime, I will slip into something."

III.

The Questionnaire,
with Claus's answers highlighted in bold.

1. Sexual taboos are:

a) absurd
b) exciting
c) subject to destruction and regeneration

2. the use of gloves and brushes during foreplay is:

a) thrilling
b) a big turn off
c) a necessary evil

3. Orgasm without intercourse is:

a) beautiful
b) ugly
c) pointless

4. I would rather have intercourse with:

a) a supermodel
b) someone who understands me emotionally
c) a book

5. Kissing is:

a) Okay
b) unnatural and sickening
c) the liberation of the arrow of the self

6. Livecasting my intercourse sessions I find to be:

a) exhilarating
b) amusing
c) embarrassing

7. My preferred length of time to engage in foreplay is:

a) less than one hour
b) between two and three hours
c) **between three and six hours**

8. During the peak of intercourse I feel:

a) as if the world had stopped moving
b) **stasis and breakdown, static and centrifugal motion that rises above matter**
c) that I must hurry

9. After intercourse I prefer to:

a) cuddle in the arms of my lover and sigh
b) revel in my sated senses and do it again
c) **read a book**

IV.

The door opened and Seshat entered. She was wearing a dark blue, seductive peignoir, with a low neckline, and decorated with black lace and see-through short sleeves. The front was tied up with a soft belt; the back was cut out, so that an ample amount of pleasant skin was revealed when she turned around.

Looking over Claus's answers on the questionnaire, she nodded her head with satisfaction.

"You have a very high hygienic value," she said quietly.

Claus nodded his head.

The truth was that, though he was normally a man of exceptional sang froid, this woman had begun to make him nervous. Yes, he had, from his youth onward, had countless adventures of amour—with dwarfs and giantesses, librettos and compendiums, psychic healers and tantric masseuses. He had toured the most aloof brothels of Mae Sot and taken up romantic correspondence with women in Chechnya and those in Justizvollzugsanstalt Schwäbisch Gmünd, and that of Aichach. But this woman . . . there was something different about her.

"Are you ready?" she asked.

"*Jah.*"

"Give me the book, Claus."

"It is better if I retain it."

"Claus . . ."

"*Ach, wir kennen uns wenig . . .*"

"*Denn es waltet ein Geist in uns . . .*"

Her eyes became extraordinarily bright. Claus felt himself mesmerized, seduced, taken over. He longed for this creature as he had never longed for anything in his life. He wished to reach out to her. But he could not move.

"Do you believe in love, Claus? Do you remember me? . . . Do you remember the Mistress? . . ."

He wished he could speak, but no sound would come from his lips.

"Now we can play," she murmured, taking from her breast a dark blue blindfold with black floral lace and a small bow with a pendant on the front. She relaxed the blindfold over his eyes. He could no longer see.

"*Je suis la maîtresse . . . de la maison . . . des livres . . .*"

He felt a violent jab to his left arm. Then a profound dizziness; the shadow world.

V.

He opened his eyes.

The world was new. Giant flowers spread their petals, which were pages, in pink and green, on which Uranian verse was displayed in purple and sepia inks. Serpentine streams wound into the distance—yet they were not streams at all, but unrolled scrolls on which gurgled endless tales, quaint and curious, sweet and strong . . . And in those environs naked women were doing headstands and, thus, in that profound position reading first edition copies of *Der Golem* and *Das Glasperlenspiel* upside down; and lads, also naked, instead of walking, cartwheeled towards their destinations, which were bibliotecas and librerias, hedonistic reading rooms and sumptuous athenaeums. Great temples loomed up, each one constructed of a million rare volumes, spires stretching into the clouds; and the pathways were paved with exquisite bindings.

Delighted, Claus wandered forward, towards one of those structures, which he arrived at in no less time than it takes to recite a haiku by Bonchō. Two doors, shaped and illustrated like the boards of the 1904 edition of Karl

Hans Strobl's *Die Eingebungen des Arphaxat* swung open of their own accord, and our hero entered, and within, arrayed on pedestals and shelves, racks and tables, a million works entertained his eye: the rarest tracts and monographs, opuscules, treatises and weighty tomes.

There were books printed on glass, bindings of butterfly wings with pages whip-stitched with spiders' silk, and others again, which, instead of ink were printed with elephant semen, morning dew, or peacocks' tears. Other books were in the form of large bowls of cream on which elaborate poems had been printed in jam-juice; while others, meant for cyclopses and titans, were printed on giant blocks of cement and bound between enormous sheets of iron.

There were volumes printed on razor blades, which cut the hands when those pages were turned, staining it with the reader's blood.

One of the most delightful objects was a little pamphlet, the pages of which were mustard seeds, and it was bound between two grains of brown rice, and Claus was bending over it and examining it with a magnifying glass that was by its side, when suddenly he realized he was being spoken to.

He looked up.

A bearded individual with a strong Norwegian accent was talking to him.

"Yes, yes," this latter said, "I understand perfectly. When I was first chairman of the *Bibliofiklubben*, we had several cases such as yours and we all know that Paul Botten-Hansen was just such a one. . ."

"*Jah?*" Claus murmured uncertainly.

"*Jah, jah.* His virility was, just as yours is, inexplicably linked to books. He often grasped the 1685 edition of the *Taare-Offer* while engaging in the conjugal act, quoting,

> *"Langt meere rørdte ham med Hierted end*
> > *med Haanden*
> *Søg HErren, Menniske, saa hand din Andact*
> > *seer,*
> *Det er da lige got paa hvilcken Stæd det skeer.*

"and this filled him with the most violent pleasures . . . At other times he made his wife place an open copy of Baron von Holberg's *Morals Kierne* between her legs in order to stimulate his interest."

"The 1716 edition?" Claus inquired.

"Naturally—in imperial folio, bound in blood-colored morocco."

"How could that not induce interest!"

"Yes . . . And then there is the case of George Spencer-Churchill, the 5th Duke of Marlborough . . . In conversation with others, at the mere mention of some rare volume, he would blush and become aroused. When he would visit prostitutes, which he did frequently, he would bring with him a suitcase full of the rarest books and introduce them into their amorous play . . . Possessed of a thousand dozen volumes, at home he would hide books under the pillows and mattress, their mere presence helping him in his matrimonial duties with Lady Susan Stewart, and thus their four children owed their existence as much to the charms of his library, as to those of their mother . . . But with the Duke excess followed excess and he eventually abandoned all congress with his spouse, choosing instead for his constant amorous devotions the pearly white pages of Valderfen's edition of Boccaccio's *Decameron* which he had purchased for a staggering £2,260 at the Duke of Roxburgh's sale in 1812!"

Claus became thoughtful. What this man was saying sounded a bit too familiar.

"Can you not see the reason why it is predominately men who sojourn themselves to book collecting?"

A confused look beset the face of Claus.

"I . . ." he said.

"Yes, you. You. You look at books. But what are you looking at? Is it not, after all, the two spread legs of the female? Is it not, after all, nothing more than a sexual aberration? Or, maybe, maybe, not an aberration at all—but simply a longing to once again enter the womb from whence you came . . . Just as a book cannot live long without being bound, so the mind of a man cannot flourish without vision and whimsy . . . but with some of us (unfortunate, fortunate?), whimsy transforms itself into an unnatural phenomenon—the sea boils, the skies collapse!"

Just then a smallish man with a white wig approached them.

"Have you seen my Aeschylus?" he asked. "My *Tragoediae septem* of 1552 seems to have gone missing."

"Ah, Herr Reusch, there you are. We have a visitor."

The other looked at Claus with glassy eyes. "My Aeschylus . . ." he murmured.

"This one would scarcely have seen it," said the first man, "for his perversion is so extreme that he only buys books printed in Romania and his own decadent city of Düsseldorf."

"Yes, he appears to be somewhat tainted."

"All of us suffer to some degree . . ."

"It is true. I never could engage in amour without touching my Aeschylus. Even calling it up in my imagination makes me tremble . . . When I was a lad I would take books, hide in the closet with them, and do unspeakable things."

"That is how a good binding gets ruined."

"My Aeschylus is possessed of every charm . . . and I cannot hold it without anxious excitement . . ."

"*Meine Brüder*," Claus said in a sentimental voice.

"You wish to confess?" said the first man.

"Tell us . . . of your difficulty," said the second.

And then Claus, after inhaling deeply as if he were about to dive into liquid depths, spoke:

"Where and when did I become infected with this *schreckliche Krankheit*, this bibliomania which, to keep at bay, has gobbled up all my resources? . . . At school, age nine, Frau Schrobsdorff. *Jah, jah*, she taught us many things. Her ears were very white; when she leaned over, a delicate and unique odor, like that of Russian leather, filled my nostrils. I felt at harmony with that woman. Every day she would read to the class from *Der schwarze Mustang*, by Karl May. The *exemplar* of the book, large and hardbound, published by the Union Deutsche Verlagsgesellschaft in 1899, sat on her lap and thus my gaze was drawn there. At night I only dreamed of this; had the most pronounced fantasies of being entirely covered by the books pages . . . of feeling their pressure and touch . . . Then I found myself suddenly filled with a new *Begeisterung* —a great desire—to possess a copy of *Der schwarze Mustang* for myself. Through my tears and tantrums I convinced my parents to acquire for me further volumes—*Der Schatz im Silbersee, Das Vermächtnis des Inka, Die Sklavenkarawane*. And so my monotheistic attraction was born, and it grew ever stronger until I reached mature manhood, when, with perverse pleasure, I put books at the foremost order of my lusts, above statues and armpits, whippings and rubbings, feet and furs . . . and, yes, even women . . . For what woman could ever have the magnificence and beauty of a finely bound volume? Could her skin ever compete in softness with the velum fly-leaves, or her back be firmer than the thick boards of a fine cover?

"Oh, *mein Gott*, how many volumes I have fondled, caressed, kissed and sucked! How many desired *exemplars* have caused me sleeplessness and inner torture! . . . Ah, and for them I would commit criminal acts, consummate my lust with them in public, be imprisoned, have my toe-nails and teeth torn out, be shredded by iron machines, have my blood coarse like a river through the streets! . . . My sensual feelings . . . of delight . . . enwrapping myself in luxuriant pages of pleasure . . . oh . . . my head it turns heavy . . . my thoughts . . ."

IV.

When Claus awoke he was at a bus stop on the Luegplatz. It was early morning and the air had with it a chill. The pants he was wearing were his own, but the shirt, oddly enough, was not. He felt wretched, as if he had spent the night beneath a demolition hammer—his head in pieces.

He looked from right to left, up and down, but his Zacharias Werner book was nowhere in sight.

"Why does this sort of thing always happen after a Little Annie concert?" he murmured.

Just then the bus pulled up and the driver gave him a skeptical look.

"*Diese entarteten . . .* " the driver murmured as Claus climbed on board.

Forty-five minutes later he was at his house.

When he approached his door he noticed a large package wrapped in brown paper sitting there. A note was attached to it with a piece of Tesafilm. It read:

BELIEVE IN LOVE.

When he took the package inside and opened it, he discovered a giant brass *Schwanz*.

About the Authors

James Champagne is the author of the collections *Grimoire: A Compendium of Neo-Goth Narratives* (2012) and *Autopsy of an Eldritch City: Ten Tales of Strange & Unproductive Thinking* (2015), both published by Rebel Satori Press. He has also written two novels, *Confusion* (self-published, 2006) and *Harlem Smoke* (Snuggly Books, 2019). His work has appeared in the anthologies *Userlands: New Fiction Writers From the Blogging Underground*, *Mighty in Sorrow: a Tribute to Current 93 & David Tibet*, and *Marked to Die: A Tribute to Mark Samuels*. He was born in 1980 and lives in Rhode Island.

Brendan Connell was born in Santa Fe, New Mexico, in 1970. His works of fiction include *Unpleasant Tales* (Eibonvale Press, 2013), *The Architect* (PS Publishing, 2012), *Lives of Notorious Cooks* (Chômu Press, 2012), *Miss Homicide Plays the Flute* (Eibonvale Press, 2013), *Jottings from a Far Away Place* (Snuggly Books, 2015), and *Cannibals of West Papua* (Zagava, 2015).

Quentin S. Crisp was born in 1972, in North Devon, U.K. He studied Japanese at Durham University and graduated in the year 2000. From 2001 to 2003, he did research in Japanese literature, on a Monbushô Scholarship, at Kyôto University. He has had fiction and poetry published by Tartarus Press, PS Publishing, Eibonvale Press, Snuggly Books and others. He currently resides in Bexleyheath, is editor for Chômu Press and is studying for an MA in philosophy at Birkbeck College.

Justin Isis has lived in Tokyo for close to ten years. His collections include *I Wonder What Human Flesh Tastes Like* (2011) and *Welcome to the Arms Race* (2016) from Chômu Press, and the forthcoming *Pleasant Tales II* from Snuggly Books, as well as the poetry collection *Divorce Procedures For the Hairdressers of a Metallic and Inconstant Goddess* (2016). He has previously edited Chômu Press's *Dadaoism* anthology (2012), and *Marked to Die: A Tribute to Mark Samuels* (Snuggly Books). His stories have appeared in *Postscripts* and a number of anthologies.

Damian Murphy is the author of *The Imperishable Sacraments*, *Seduction of the Golden Pheasant*, and *Abyssinia*, among other collections and novellas. His work has been published on the Mount Abraxas, Les Éditions de L'Oubli, and L'Homme Récent imprints of Ex Occidente Press, in Bucharest, and by Zagava Books, in Dusseldorf. His latest collection, published by Snuggly Books in September of 2017, and the first to be offered in a paperback edition, is entitled *Daughters of Apostasy*. He was born and lives in Seattle, Washington.

A PARTIAL LIST OF SNUGGLY BOOKS

G. ALBERT AURIER *Elsewhere and Other Stories*
JULES BARBEY D'AUREVILLY *Hannibal's Ring*
S. HENRY BERTHOUD *Misanthropic Tales*
LÉON BLOY *The Tarantulas' Parlor and Other Unkind Tales*
ÉLÉMIR BOURGES *The Twilight of the Gods*
JAMES CHAMPAGNE *Harlem Smoke*
FÉLICIEN CHAMPSAUR *The Latin Orgy*
FÉLICIEN CHAMPSAUR
 The Emerald Princess and Other Decadent Fantasies
BRENDAN CONNELL *Clark*
BRENDAN CONNELL *Unofficial History of Pi Wei*
RAFAELA CONTRERAS *The Turquoise Ring and Other Stories*
ADOLFO COUVE *When I Think of My Missing Head*
QUENTIN S. CRISP *Aiaigasa*
QUENTIN S. CRISP *Graves*
LADY DILKE *The Outcast Spirit and Other Stories*
CATHERINE DOUSTEYSSIER-KHOZE *The Beauty of the Death Cap*
ÉDOUARD DUJARDIN *Hauntings*
BERIT ELLINGSEN *Now We Can See the Moon*
BERIT ELLINGSEN *Vessel and Solsvart*
ENRIQUE GÓMEZ CARRILLO *Sentimental Stories*
EDMOND AND JULES DE GONCOURT *Manette Salomon*
REMY DE GOURMONT *From a Faraway Land*
GUIDO GOZZANO *Alcina and Other Stories*
EDWARD HERON-ALLEN *The Complete Shorter Fiction*
RHYS HUGHES *Cloud Farming in Wales*
J.-K. HUYSMANS *Knapsacks*
COLIN INSOLE *Valerie and Other Stories*
JUSTIN ISIS *Pleasant Tales II*
JUSTIN ISIS (editor) *Marked to Die: A Tribute to Mark Samuels*
JUSTIN ISIS AND DANIEL CORRICK (editors)
 Drowning in Beauty: The Neo-Decadent Anthology